ACROSS THE HIGH DIVIDE

When Bodie goes after Ty McLennan, it has nothing to do with money. McLennan shot and killed Bodie's friend, Gunnar Olsen, during a bank robbery. When Bodie attends the funeral, he meets US Marshal Alvin LeRoy. LeRoy is also on the trail of McLennan and his bunch, so they decide to team up and track them down together. But as always, the final showdown could go one of two ways. Bodie could exact revenge for his murdered friend . . . or join him on Boot Hill!

NEIL HUNTER

ACROSS THE HIGH DIVIDE

Complete and Unabridged

LINFORD
Leicester

First published in Great Britain in 2017

First Linford Edition
published 2018

Copyright © 2017 by Neil Hunter
All rights reserved

A catalogue record for this book is available
from the British Library.

ISBN 978–1–4448–3726–1

Published by
F. A. Thorpe (Publishing)
Anstey, Leicestershire

Set by Words & Graphics Ltd.
Anstey, Leicestershire
Printed and bound in Great Britain by
T. J. International Ltd., Padstow, Cornwall

This book is printed on acid-free paper

KENT
ARTS & LIBRARIES

In 1872, the Supreme Court ruled that bounty hunters were a part of the U.S. law enforcement system with the decision that:

'When the bail is given, the principal is regarded as delivered to the custody of his sureties. Their domain is a continuance of the original imprisonment. Whenever they choose to do so, they may seize him and deliver him up to his discharge; and if it cannot be done at once, they may imprison him until it can be done. They may exercise their rights in person or by agent. They may pursue him into another state; may arrest him on the Sabbath; and if necessary, may break and enter his house for that purpose. The seizure is not made by virtue of due

1

process. None is needed. It is likened to the arrest by the Sheriff of an escaped prisoner.'

CLEAR SPRINGS — EAST
OF THE DIVIDE

'Man that is born of a woman hath but a short time to live, and is full of misery. He cometh up, and is cut down, like a flower; he fleeth as it were a shadow, and never continueth in one stay. In the midst of life we are in death: of whom may we seek for succor, but of thee, O Lord, who for our sins art justly displeased? Yet, O Lord God most holy, O Lord most mighty, O holy and most merciful Savior, deliver us not into the bitter pains of eternal death. Thou knowest, Lord, the secrets of our hearts; shut not thy merciful ears to our prayer; but spare us, Lord most holy, O God most mighty, O holy and merciful Savior, thou most worthy Judge eternal, suffer us not, at our last hour, for

3

any pains of death, to fall from thee.'

Wasn't it enough a man had to die without having such depressing words spoken over his grave? Bodie thought. He heard what the minister was saying but felt the words were unnecessarily gloomy. He was not a religious man himself, finding too much darkness in the delivered words, and the visions of an afterlife that didn't hold out too much promise.

Overhead, the sky had a leaden look to it, and a dry wind was blowing in across the landscape. Gritty dust blew against the cemetery's headstones and tugged at clothes. Bodie hunched his shoulders against the wind. He was holding his hat in his hands, pulled to his chest, his head bent forward. He was dressed in black, even down to a black shirt and string tie, and that was purely a mark of respect for the departed . . .

★   ★   ★

Gunnar Olsen, the sheriff of Clear Springs, had been a friend of Bodie's for some time. Olson had been a lawman for many years — a solid, dependable man who had forsaken carrying a gun in the last five years of his life. His decision caused a deal of debate around Clear Springs, and some open criticism, but Olson refused to back down. His choice proved to be sound. The town had never been overly rowdy, the only exceptions being when local ranch hands came in at month's end, and sometimes weekends, to let off steam and spend their pay in the local saloons and restaurants. When trouble did show itself, Gunnar Olsen would step in and settle it either with words, or if things became a little stressed, his fists.

Olsen had been a big man, in all respects, standing over six feet tall, with a powerful build. With thick blond hair and blue eyes, he had been good-looking as well, and his deep voice still held the cadence of his Swedish background, despite having lived in America since he was five years old. He had become a lawman simply because he had a deep feeling for maintaining it. Prior to pinning on a badge, Olsen had been a skilled wheelwright, running a successful business in Clear Springs. When he was offered the position of deputy, he had immediately accepted the job, siding the then sheriff, Rafe Thomas. In the five years he was deputy, Olsen maintained his business; and when he was elected full-time lawman on Thomas's retirement, he divided his time between his business and the law.

From day one, Olsen put his mark on the way he ran the sheriff's office. He was a hands-on lawman, working day and night to keep the town safe. He was unmarried and devoted himself to his chosen way of life. His stern but fair way quickly earned him the respect of the community. He only had to show his face when trouble reared its head to have those involved back down. Olsen had a natural affinity for dealing with anyone stepping out of line. It was inevitable he would come up against those who wanted to step over the line, and anyone who did face the big lawman soon found they had taken on more than was sensible. Olsen talked his way out of trouble on more than one occasion, despite sometimes having to face someone with a gun. If his words didn't do the trick, Olsen's big fists would end the dispute quickly. Though this seemed to be a satisfactory way, there were those who were vocal in their opposition. They felt Olsen was walking a fine line, and one day something would happen he wouldn't be able to deal with.

In the end, their fears were proven to be correct.

When Ty McLennan showed up in Clear Springs — a thirty-five-year-old who could talk his way out of anything, seemingly looking for work and proving to the town he was a handy man to have around — he sided with Olsen during a situation in one of the town's saloons. A trio of out-of-town drifters had been causing problems, and it was one of the few times Gunnar Olsen found himself close to being outnumbered. Olsen had tried to calm the ruckus down; but already having drunk too much, the newcomers had refused to back down, and Olsen found himself being threatened by a drawn gun in the hand of a belligerent, loudmouthed opponent. It might have gone badly for Olsen if it had not been for McLennan stepping in, swinging an unexpected fist that had forced the gunman to his knees. Although the troublemaker lost his gun, he rounded on McLennan, and they traded blows. By this time, Olsen had seen he was out from under the gun, and was able to deal with the other pair in his usual manner. It was over in minutes. The three rowdies were floored, their weapons taken away; and with McLennan's help Olsen dragged them over to the jail and locked them in the cells.

There seemed an inevitability to what happened next. The town fathers convened a hasty meeting, which resulted in the suggestion to appoint McLennan as deputy sheriff. Olsen had to admit he had been placed in a difficult position, and if McLennan had not been there a tragedy might have occurred. Ty McLennan became deputy sheriff and slipped into the role with ease. Yet there was something about his new assistant that unsettled Gunnar Olsen. He couldn't put his finger on it, and kept his thoughts to himself, but watched and waited because he was sure there was more to the man.

Over the next couple of weeks, McLennan took to his new job with enthusiasm, backing Olsen whenever the need arose. It seemed on the surface that the town's new deputy was fitting in nicely. Even Olsen couldn't find fault with the man's behavior, yet he still held a lingering doubt that he could not dismiss.

With roundup time bringing in extra

hands for the outlying ranches, new faces kept appearing in Clear Springs, and the influx meant busier times when hungry and thirsty men came to town, especially at weekends. The saloons — all four — found themselves busy, and none of them were complaining. They stayed open late, as did the couple of restaurants along the main street.

It was to be expected that trouble would show itself. Cowhands worked hard and played hard. They came to town determined to have a good time. Liquor flowed. So did emotions, which had to bust free, leading to fallouts. The majority ended amicably over another round of drinks. Some men stepped over the line, however, and whiskey-fueled tempers erupted. Blows were thrown. Some missed their mark. Others did not.

★   ★   ★

It was mid-morning. The early rush was past so the bank was quiet. There was only one customer when Ty McLennan walked in, nodding at the tellers behind the counter. His appearance was accepted. He had been doing this for weeks, his armed presence a comfort as the big safe behind the counter held money awaiting the monthly payday for the local ranches and the timber company situated a few miles out of town in the hills. Additional cash had been shipped in a few days earlier, arriving at the Clear Springs rail depot two days ago. Added to the money already in the safe, it came to a tidy sum.

McLennan stood quietly near the main window, shotgun in one hand, muzzle down as Levi Benjamin crossed to the safe and began open it. It had been Benjamin, one of the town council members, who suggested an extra safeguard at the bank. Benjamin was a nervous man where large amounts of money were concerned, and he was also one of the most vociferous when it came to voicing his worry over the way

Gunnar Olsen ran the sheriff's office. The fact that nothing had ever happened to cause any risk didn't sit well with the pale-skinned man, who spent his days worrying over every operation within the bank; and his being a prominent official, his word carried a great deal of weight. Ever one to maintain peace and tranquility, Olsen had agreed to his employer's concerns and gave his new deputy the job of overseeing the distribution of the various payroll distributions that occurred at the end of each month. This had the effect of keeping everyone happy, especially the needy Levi Benjamin.

The lone customer, transaction completed, left the bank, and McLennan closed the door behind him. Before he completed that action, he faced across the street, free hand reaching up to touch the brim of his hat. That done, he turned and resumed his position beside the door, shotgun at his side again — the difference was he had eared back both hammers.

Benjamin and his chief teller were hauling open the heavy safe door. The other two employees, at their posts, were ready to start counting out the various payrolls. All the attention was on that, so none of them even noticed the fleeting shadows that passed across the plate-glass window of the bank, or the door being quietly opened to admit two men, who stepped inside in response to Ty McLennan's signal. By the time their presence was known, the newcomers had placed themselves, spaced apart, where they could cover the rear section of the bank. McLennan had moved close to the counter, raising the shotgun and casually aiming it.

It was Benjamin himself, turning to speak, who saw the twin-barreled weapon. Pale features became even paler as he saw the shogun.

'What is this, deputy?'

'This is a holdup,' McLennan said. 'You do as you're told and no one gets hurt. Do something stupid, and . . . '

McLennan nodded at his partners.

13

They moved quickly behind the counter, pulling out the folded canvas bags they had under their coats. Without a word, or wasted motion, they went to the open safe and dragged out the stacks of bank-notes, quickly filling the canvas bags. They ignored the bagged coins because they would simply add weight.

'We're done.'

McLennan's partners moved to the door, bulging sacks in their left hands, leaving gun hands clear.

Levi Benjamin rushed forward, color flooding his face. 'You can't do this,' he said. 'All that money . . . McLennan . . . I spoke up for you . . . '

'Damn right you did, and I figure you won't do it again. Make you think next time.'

His right hand dropped to the big Colt on his hip. He drew it quick and smooth and slammed it brutally across the side of Benjamin's face. Bone cracked and flesh was split. The banker slumped to the floor, blood streaming down his cheek.

'Let's go, boys. Just step out nice and easy. Horses at the hitch rail right by us. We ride out steady.'

As they emerged from the bank into the clear light, no one even noticed. McLennan let his partners walk just ahead, towards the three horses waiting for them.

The raised voice carried across the street from behind McLennan.

'They robbed the bank!'

McLennan turned, seeing the white face of one of the bank's tellers. He was framed in the open doorway, eyes wide with raw fear as he realized the position he had placed himself in. Before he could pull back, McLennan lifted the shotgun and shot him in the face. The close impact of the twelve-gauge, the full charge barely having time to spread, blew the man's head apart. He fell back, the bloody maw of flesh and bone all that was left.

'Let's go,' McLennan said.

Their peaceful retreat was shot to hell now. All they could do was get out

15

of Clear Springs while the chance still remained.

McLennan's partners reached their horses, swinging into saddles and looping the money bags from their saddle horns.

'*Go . . .* '

They spurred their way along the street, scattering anyone who happened to step in their way. One woman was sent to the ground as she was run down.

McLennan was reaching to mount when he heard the voice he knew so well.

It was Gunnar Olsen. He had been heading for the bank when he witnessed the three men step out. Saw McLennan gun down the teller.

In that moment, he realized his misgivings about Ty McLennan had been correct. But none of that mattered right now. He was the law in Clear Springs, and it was down to him to stop McLennan.

'Ty . . . I can't let you . . . '

There was a moment when their eyes met and Olsen saw the cold, dead expression of a man he didn't recognize.

'Dumb sonofabitch, what you going to do? Talk me to death?' McLennan expelled a chill laugh. 'Lawdog with no damn gun. What the hell do you expect . . . '

And with no more feeling than stepping on a bug, Ty McLennan put his remaining shot into Olsen's chest at close range, the same as he had done with the luckless bank teller. Olsen fell back, face registering shock and surprise. He slammed down on the boardwalk, body shuddering in reaction as his system was overwhelmed by the blast. The last thing he ever saw was McLennan's bleak expression as he swung into his saddle and turned away.

By the time any kind of response was raised, McLennan and his partners had thundered out of town, and all the shocked inhabitants could do was stare at the two dead men and wonder at the unexpected and violent events that had been visited on the quiet town of Clear Springs.

⋆   ⋆   ⋆

Bodie's arrival in town went virtually unnoticed. As soon as he had collected his horse from the train's box car, he led it to the livery stable, giving orders for it to be well cared for, then took his possibles and saddlebags and sought out Clear Springs' best hotel. He had wired ahead for a room, went straight up to it and settled in. He took out his dark suit and hung it from the hook on the wall in the hope the creases might not look so bad. He unstrapped his gunbelt and draped it over the end of the bed, then leaned his rifle against the wall. Next he sluiced water from the jug on the washstand over his face. He could feel the stubble on his jaw and decided a visit to the barber shop was called for. Opening the window to allow a little fresh air into the room, he stared out on the street as he toweled his face dry. He could see the frontage of the sheriff's office from his window.

'Damn it all to hell,' he said.

He was not going to see Gunnar Olsen's tall blond-haired figure step out, his face showing its pleasant expression. Not this time. Never again. He flung the towel aside, crossed to the bed and snatched up his gunrig, strapping it on. He found himself checking the Colt. Five loaded cartridges. An empty one under the hammer. Something Olsen never had to do. Not that it would have saved him anyhow. From what Bodie had learned, Gunnar Olsen hadn't even been given the chance to defend himself.

Bodie walked out of the hotel and located the barber shop. The barber recognized him from one of his infrequent visits to Clear Spring. Usually a genial, chattering individual, this time he was sober.

'Sad reason to be having to visit town, Mister Bodie.'

Bodie dropped into the chair as the towel was fastened around his neck. He stared into the mirror as the barber lathered him, sensing his customer was not in a talkative mood. He was starting in with razor when Bodie finally spoke.

'McLennan. What do you know about him?'

'Not a deal to tell. He showed up in town. Kind of helped Gunnar out over at the saloon down the street. Seemed nice enough. Made himself known to folk in town. All was going well until . . . '

'Until he turned around and bit the town in the ass. Shot down Gunnar and one of the bank tellers.'

'Gave Levi Benjamin a pistol whipping too. And his partners run down Amy Pelham on their way out of town. Broke both legs and cracked her ribs.'

Bodie stared at his own reflection in the mirror. He was thinking about Gunnar Olsen. He hadn't been this way in a while. Too much business keeping him at a distance. Olsen had been a longtime friend. Though they were opposites in the way they viewed handling lawbreakers, they had struck up a lasting association; and whenever Bodie had been close to Clear Springs, he made it a point to call in and see Olsen. The moment he heard about the man's death, the day after it happened, he caught the next available train to Clear Springs.

The door opened and a tubby figure blocked out the sun.

'Mister Bodie?'

'That's me.'

'Mister Benjamin wants to see you.'

'I'll be right along soon as I'm done here.'

The tubby man bobbed his head. 'He said he'd like for you to come before the funeral.'

'He want me to come along covered in lather?'

'I guess not.'

Bodie nodded to the barber, who had paused and gave him a nod.

'Benjamin at the bank?'

'Yessir.'

'You trot on back, boy, and I'll be there.'

After the tubby figure withdrew, Bodie glanced at the barber. 'I suppose he expects everyone to jump when he whistles?'

'Yep. He gets kind of disappointed if folk don't.'

'Considering Gunnar Olsen got killed, I don't think Mister Benjamin's at the head of the queue for being considered that important today.'

★   ★   ★

Levi Benjamin's office had an aura that befitted his importance. A thick carpet and dark wood paneling. A couple of oil paintings featuring stern men in high collars and bushy sideburns. The massive desk behind which Benjamin sat faced a line of hard-backed chairs. Four chairs on which sat four equally stiff-faced well-dressed men.

Levi Benjamin, his head bandaged to

protect the wound he had received during the robbery, watched Bodie as he stepped into the office.

'Good of you to come, Bodie,' he said, pale, thin lips held in a disapproving line.

'Hard to resist your invitation. So what can I do for you?'

Benjamin made a quick introduction of the four seated men. They nodded their acknowledgment of his presence.

'I'll make this brief,' Benjamin said. He pushed an envelope across the desk and gestured for Bodie to pick it up. 'There's over fifteen thousand dollars in there. Every man in this room has contributed. Should be adequate for your services.'

Bodie made no move to pick up the package. He simply waited, letting the silence drag on.

'Well?' Benjamin said. 'We don't have time to drag this out. We have a funeral to attend.'

'I was starting to wonder if you'd forgotten.'

'Damn you, sir.' The speaker was an overweight, flush-faced man wearing a dark suit that struggled to hide his corpulent form. He twisted his head round to glare at Bodie. 'You dare speak to us in such a manner?'

'Sure. I don't know who you are, and I don't favor the way you called me here like a damn servant.'

'You . . . '

'I don't work for you, mister, so quit the high-handed attitude.'

'Time is wasting,' Benjamin said. 'Those men are getting further away with every minute that passes.' He tapped the envelope with bony fingers. 'Why aren't you leaving?'

'Like you said yourself, there's a funeral to attend.'

'Damnit,' the overweight man said, 'do we have to listen to this . . . bounty hunter?' He picked up the envelope and thrust it at Bodie. 'Here, take the money and do your job.'

Bodie's right hand swung around and smashed the envelope from the man's hand. It spun over and over, hitting the floor, bursting open to scatter the banknotes across the carpet.

'You figure you can wave a bundle of money in my face and I'm going to jump? Mister, like I said, I don't know you and you sure as hell *don't* know me.'

The man sank back in his seat, turning his face away from Bodie.

'I don't understand,' Benjamin said. 'Isn't our money good enough for you?'

'You really expect me to take money from you? Damn right I'm going after McLennan. But not for any bounty.'

'Then why?'

'We're burying the reason today. You remember? Gunnar Olsen. He's the reason I came to Clear Springs. He was my friend.'

Bodie let the words hang as he turned and walked out of Benjamin's office.

★   ★   ★

25

He stood over the grave, staring down at the plain wood coffin; and try as he might, Bodie found it hard to recall Gunnar Olsen's face. Around him, the mourners were dispersing, leaving the manhunter on his own. The breeze stirred again, more dust sifting across the graveyard.

Ashes to ashes, dust to dust.

Seemed to sum up a man's brief existence.

Bodie's hands curled around the brim of the hat he held. He had heard something about a gathering in town where the last words would be said before Gunnar Olsen was allowed to rest. Bodie had no intention of showing up. He had paid *his* respects to his friend, and that was enough.

He sensed someone nearby. Bodie glanced up, saw the lean black-clad man standing to one side, and recognized him as one of the four who had been in Benjamin's office. Rafe Connolly. He ran the largest hardware store in town. Supplied most anything anyone could need, from simple nails through clothing and food. Bodie had met him a couple of times and found him a pleasant enough man.

'Levi is under the impression money can solve any problem,' Connolly said. 'I told him not to offer you a bounty. He doesn't understand loyalty to a friend. Mainly because he doesn't really have any himself.'

'Man can't help being who he is.'

'Gunnar did Clear Springs a great service. Ran the sheriff's office his way, and it worked.' A smile edged the man's lips. 'A lawman who went unarmed. You couldn't make it up.'

Bodie smiled. That was Gunnar. No fuss. No bother. Just a man who made his stand and refused to back down.

'You'll be leaving town now?'

'McLennan has a good start,' Bodie said. 'I need to pick up his trail before it disappears.'

'Can you do that after all this time?' Connolly said. 'I mean . . . well . . . I guess so. It is what you do, Mister Bodie.'

They made their way towards town, an easy silence between them.

'Call in at the store before you leave,' Connolly said as they reached the main street. 'Let me at least offer you supplies. No money. Just things for the trail. The least I can do. No offense intended.'

'None taken, and thanks.'

Connolly reached his store and Bodie continued along the street. When he drew level with Gunnar's office, he saw that the door was open and someone was moving around inside. Bodie stepped up on the boardwalk and walked inside.

'Been wondering when you would show up,' a familiar voice said.

The owner straightened up from where he was bending over the office desk.

It was US Marshal Alvin LeRoy.

* * *

They knew each other from brief encounters in the past. Bodie's reputation was well-documented, and though there could have been animosity coming from LeRoy, the marshal held a grudging respect for the bounty man. LeRoy was known as a tough, uncompromising lawman who had little tolerance for anyone who broke the law. They shook hands, LeRoy glancing around the office.

'He kept a tight ship,' he said. 'Never seen a lawman's office so tidy.'

'Yeah, that was Gunnar.'

'Word is you're going after Ty McLennan.'

'That going to be a problem?'

'Hell, no. Sooner that *hombre* is caught, the better. And the two who run with him.'

'Now that sounds like you might know about them.'

'Ty McLennan. His partners have been with him nigh on three years. Been playing their damn game in Texas, Kansas and New Mexico. McLennan always goes in first. Plays friendly while he figures out his plan. Has a winning way, and folk trust him. His partners drift into town once he has everything worked out. McLennan sets the time, and they hit hard and fast. None too particular who gets hurt. They're down for close on eight killings.'

'Who are his partners?'

'Marty Bell and Roy Krupps. Handy with their guns. Too handy. Bad characters. I don't see them living to an old age.'

'Heard the name Krupps,' Bodie said. 'Not the other.'

'If you ever met them, they're not the kind you forget.'

ALONG THE DIVIDE

Being unshaven and wearing the same clothes they had on their backs since leaving Clear Springs had done little to improve Marty Bell's mood. He had a reputation for being dissatisfied with most things on the trail, and the fact they had been riding more or less continuously since the day of the robbery did little to ease his discomfort. He shared his feelings with McLennan and Krupps until they became truly tired of his grousing.

'Damnation, Marty, will you just shut your mouth,' Krupps said. 'All I hear is you moaning. It's the same for all of us.'

Bell twisted in his saddle, throwing a scowl at his partner. 'I still say we should ease off some. Ain't no posse on our back trail. Hell, that pissant town couldn't raise a cheer, less a bunch of yokels to chase us.'

'You certain sure about that?' McLennan said. 'We're goin' to look foolish if they come boilin' over them hills anytime.'

'I don't think so.'

McLennan hooked a leg across his saddle horn and took his time fashioning a smoke. He struck a match across the heel of his boot, lit up and drew smoke in deep.

'Next couple of days we'll be across the divide. Nice quiet ride in front of us.' He jabbed a finger in the direction of the craggy slopes and peaks that formed a barrier in front of them. 'Other side and we're in the clear. No point gettin' ourselves in a sweat.'

'I still say . . . ' Bell continued.

'Yeah, yeah, we all heard what you have to say,' Krupps snapped. 'Hell, Marty, I can hear your voice when I'm asleep.'

McLennan smiled. Bell and Krupps were prone to these endless verbal squabbles. It was in their nature. Any stranger would have figured they were enemies, but wasn't so. Come the day, they would stand back to back in order to ward off a physical threat. Anyone who had faced them — if they survived — would see the way they worked together. It would take a good man to put them down. Men had tried and were buried because they misread the signs.

In the business they pursued, these men had to depend on their partners. They had an unwritten code that bound them together. They sided with each other, through good times and bad, and it was the closest they came to being honorable men. Outlaws they might have been; unruly and violent, with a disregard for what others might term respectability. But Bell and Krupps would never even consider doing anything to break the bond that kept them together.

By the time McLennan had finished his cigarette, Bell and Krupps had talked themselves out. Krupps slid from his horse and adjusted his saddle, then ran his hands over the animal's legs. Satisfied there were no problems, he stood by, stretching the knots out of his spine.

'My ass is numb,' he said.

'Matches your damned head then,' Bell said.

They all took the opportunity to dismount and walk about. The horses used the opportunity to crop at the skinny grass around them.

'Ty, we going to stop over at Malachi's place like you told us?' Bell said.

'We have reason.'

'Such as?'

'You'll find out.'

'That sumbitch will make us pay,' Krupps said. 'Allus does.'

'He ain't in business 'cause he's all sweetness and light,' McLennan said.

'Well, hell, you got that right.'

McLennan swung himself back into the saddle and picked up his reins. 'There's a reason we need to stop over at Remson's.'

Bell hunched forward in his saddle. 'I knew you had somethin' turning over in that head of yourn. I see you going in and out that telegraph office in Clear

Springs. That to do with it?'

'Could be.'

'Could be hell. You got something going on.'

'Sooner we get to Remson's, the sooner you'll find out.'

With McLennan leading the way, Bell and Krupps lined up behind him. It would take a few more hours to reach Malachi Remson's place. On reflection, Krupps saw the sense in the visit. Maybe better to rest overnight and get a good meal down before they started on the long ride over the divide. Up this high, the weather could be unpredictable. And they needed to make sure they had everything before they moved on.

* * *

Malachi Remson's establishment offered rest and shelter, food and essentials. The policy was you could have what you wanted as long as you had the money to pay for it. Remson did not offer credit in any form. No cash — no goods. He hauled in his wares for sale by mule train or shipped in by a freight wagon, and the cost was added to the price he charged. The man asked no questions and made no differentiation between good or bad. He served all. There was no side-taking. Remson had been operating for a good few years, and in that time he had seen all kinds of men — and a few women — pass his way. It was true he charged high. Any complaints were answered by his simple philosophy that was based on, 'I didn't ask you to come. You chose to. If you don't like my way of business, you're welcome to leave.'

Remson's place lay in a wide natural basin, with a permanent creek meandering from north to south. The basin was surrounded by timbered slopes thick with green brush. It boasted a couple of grassy meadows around the creek. He had come across it by accident some years back while he was riding the high levels on the lookout for such a spot. The moment he saw it,

Remson knew he had found his place, and he set out to create his permanent outpost. There was a need for such a place that could offer rest and sustenance for people making their way across the divide as they traveled east and west.

Remson started with a simple cabin, expanding the original building when needed. The structure spread with little planning so that it became a sprawl of connected extensions. Once established, Remson started to build his livestock as well. Behind the building were hog pens and a couple of corrals. A small herd of cattle wandered across the grassy meadows, and chickens were scattered around the area. They provided fresh meat and eggs for Remson's visitors.

McLennan and his partners rode in close to noon. They scanned the open yard fronting the building prior to dismounting. There was a shaggy gray horse standing outside the corral, reins looped around one of the fence posts.

McLennan recognized the animal. He knew the rider, and as he let his thoughts gather he figured his plan was running well.

'Looks peaceful enough,' Bell said.

'That don't mean a damn thing.' Krupps slid his rifle from the saddle boot. 'Maybe too damn peaceful.'

McLennan shook his head. 'Ain't anything ever right for you?'

'He ain't happy if he cain't grumble,' Bell said.

'Got that damned right.'

They tied their horses to the hitch rail and made their way inside. It had been some long time since they had called in at Remson's. Nothing seemed to have changed in the big cluttered room. Dry goods were stacked on the floor, on the shelves, around the place. There was a crude bar fronting lines of bottles. A stove in one corner held a large metal coffee pot. A number of rough tables and wooden ladder-back chairs provided the opportunity to sit. In back was a kitchen where Remson's

Mexican helper prepared hot food.

Malachi Remson — a bluff, sturdy man sporting a thick mustache and a head of unruly brown hair — watched from his place behind the bar as the three stepped inside.

'Been a while since you boys were here,' he said.

'We been busy,' Krupps said.

'So the story goes.'

They bellied up to the bar, leaning rifles against it.

'You still brew that beer of yourn?' McLennan said.

'I do.'

McLennan laid coins on the scarred bar top. 'We'll take three.'

'You got dust to settle?'

Bell tipped his hat back. 'Some.'

Remson filled thick glasses from the barrel behind him and slid them across the bar. He watched as the amber liquid was sampled, then drained.

'Damn, I don't know what you put in that brew,' Bell said, 'but it's got a kick.'

'I should hope so,' Remson said.

'Beer with no flavor ain't beer.'

He took a dark cigar from the folds of his baggy shirt and stuck it in his mouth, found a Lucifer and scratched it across the bar. The lit cigar produced thick smoke that had a sweetish odor.

McLennan had turned his back to the bar so he was able to check out the main room. He saw two customers, one seated against the far wall facing them across the table he was seated at, a wide-brimmed soft felt hat on the table in front of him. He had a window behind him, leaving him a dark shape. Even though he couldn't see the man's face, McLennan knew who he was. He gave the still figure a brief nod of his head. Then he turned to face the other man. *He* was watching McLennan.

'That you, Caleb Murchison?' McLennan said.

Even seated, it was plain to see he was tall and bone-thin, his buckskin shirt and pants hanging loose on his frame. He stared across the room in McLennan's direction, a hollow-cheeked seamed brown face moving as he chewed on a thick wad of tobacco. Narrowed eyes stared out from hooded lids as he crossed the room. He shook his long gray-streaked hair back from his face as he closed in on McLennan.

'You still on the owlhoot?' he said, neither accusing nor praising.

'What makes you say that, Caleb?'

'Only a suspicion. I heard LeRoy's been in the area asking questions. Your names came up is all.'

A low, forceful curse burst from Krupps. He banged his beer glass down on the bar. 'Sonofabitch lawdog. Why's he askin' about us?'

'Why I cain't imagine,' Bell said. 'Must be we're more popular than we thought.'

'Now LeRoy is some dogged son,' Murchison said. 'Hell, I don't need to remind you, Ty.'

'Grateful for the notice,' McLennan said. He held up his glass. 'Take a beer with us?'

'Mighty Christian of you,' Murchison said.

41

'Lawdog. That damn lawdog,' Krupps said forcibly. 'Last thing we need is that hound on our tails.'

McLennan made no comment. A glance across at Bell was enough. Of all the US marshals who might be on the lookout, they had to draw LeRoy, a straight-arrow determined lawman who found a man's trail and was known to stick with it. LeRoy had a reputation as a man who didn't understand the notion of ever giving up. If he picked up the scent, he would follow, nose down and totally focused.

Alvin LeRoy.

What they didn't know was Bodie's presence in Clear Springs. If they had, their sense of unease would have been that much stronger.

Murchison glanced up from his beer, stroking a big hand across his mouth. 'You boys headed across the divide? Now that's a trip where you don't need to be lookin' over your shoulder.'

'We're doin' fine,' Krupps said.

'Likely we were doing fine before

hearing about LeRoy,' Bell said. He tapped McLennan on the shoulder. 'Ain't what we need right now.'

McLennan had to agree. Clearing the divide was one thing. Doing it with the chance of a lawman like Alvin LeRoy in back of them would only get in the way. And with the job McLennan had planned, the worry of LeRoy showing up had all the hallmarks of trouble.

Big trouble.

McLennan told his partners to stay where they were while he and Murchison, with the addition of a full bottle of premium whiskey and glasses, crossed to the far side of the room for a private discussion.

'What the hell is he playin' at?' Krupps said. 'Goin' all hush-mouthed with Murchison.'

'Just drink your beer, son,' Bell said. 'Ol' Ty is workin' a deal to keep that damn lawdog off our backs. He'll tell us in his own sweet time, don't you fret.'

★　★　★

'I've got a proposition for you, Caleb,' McLennan said. It had occurred to him when he had recognized the man. He filled Murchison's glass and waited as the man swallowed half.

'I'm listening.'

'It's gun work. Kind I know you done before.'

'Mebbe.'

'No need to play games. I need for you to get LeRoy off our back trail. Got a deal set up and waitin' once me and the boys get across the divide. Last thing we need is having to look over our shoulders in case that lawdog shows up.'

'US marshal ain't small potatoes, Ty.'

McLennan topped up the glass for Murchison. He was ready to make his play and knew exactly what to say.

'I'm willing to pay well.'

The gleam in Murchison's eyes was all McLennan needed to see. He was already halfway there to hooking the man.

Murchison was a hunter and trapper,

and sometime gun for hire. He roamed the territory and knew most every secret place. Where the hidden streams ran. The breeding grounds for beaver. Where the wild deer fed. But the good days for his kind were fading. Men like Murchison had to travel far and wide now. So a fistful of money couldn't be ignored. And McLennan knew Caleb Murchison of old. He had no morals when it came to earning himself easy money. The man had killed before, so it was nothing new for him.

'You ain't getting any younger,' McLennan said. 'Time to start thinking ahead.'

That amused Murchison. His seamed brown face broke into a wide grin. 'Hoss, I worked this territory since I was a sprout. Never been one to make me a permanent place. Had me a time. Money. Whiskey. Women, even. Might not seem that way to you, Ty, but I see the time this was an empty piece of country 'cept for the Indians. Now it's tending to get crowded. I'll take your offer and deal with LeRoy. Then I'll move on. Find me a quiet place where it ain't so crowded and stake myself a spot.' He drained his whiskey. 'That's what I'm doing it for, Ty. For me. Just me.'

McLennan pulled a thick roll of bank notes from his pocket and peeled off a wedge. He placed the money on the table in from of Murchison. The man laid his own big hand over the cash.

'Fair piece of money, hoss. You really must want that lawdog put down.'

'That's the way it is, Caleb. I want that feller dead and buried where nobody can find him.'

Murchison nodded, folded the money and pocketed it. 'You want his badge as a souvenir?'

'Hell, no. You bury it with him deep, so I don't ever need to be looking over my shoulder.'

'You can count on that.'

He reached for the long rifle leaning against the table, lifting it so McLennan could see it. He recognized it straight off. The 1874 Sharps was an impressive weapon, and in the right hands it became more than just a hunting rifle. With a 32-inch octagonal barrel, double-set trigger, and handling a 45–70 cartridge, the Sharps had few equals. It came with a removable Vernier sight that added to its accuracy, and could fire its powerful load an easy 1200 yards, hitting with tremendous power. It was a man-killer. A single-shot breech loader in the hands of a skilled shooter, the Sharps could maintain a continuous rate of fire. The craftsman-built falling-block action was meticulous in operation, and Caleb Murchison had reloading and firing down to a fine art.

McLennan managed a thin smile when he eyed the weapon. 'Take down LeRoy with that he won't know what hit him.'

'Damn right there, hoss. One of those 45–70 slugs will knock a man clear out of his boots before he has a chance to think about it.'

Murchison finished his drink, pulled on his hat, collected his rifle and stood.

A brief nod to McLennan was his acknowledgement of the deal. He walked out of the room without a look back. Krupps and Bell rejoined McLennan.

'You goin' to tell us now?' Krupps said.

'Figure it,' Bell said. 'He's done a deal with Murchison to get LeRoy off our trail.'

'Yeah?'

McLennan pushed the bottle of whiskey towards his partners. 'Have a drink, boys. Let's have an early wake for a certain US marshal.'

* * *

Murchison slid the Sharps into the long scabbard on the gray's right side. Before he mounted, he fished out the wad of banknotes McLennan had given him and pushed it deep inside the pouch of his saddlebags, fastening the flap securely. He swung into the saddle and tugged the horse's head round. He moved across the yard, leaving Remson's place behind.

If McLennan could have seen it, Murchison's face showed a pleased smile.

He hadn't told the man two important matters. Killing LeRoy was way more than a paid killing. It was personal; to do with family — the murder, in Murchison's way of thinking, of his sister's boy. LeRoy claimed it as a lawful kill while doing his duty. Murchison saw it different, and nothing would ever change that. Getting paid to kill LeRoy was an added bonus. Yes, he was being *paid* to kill LeRoy, a task he would have undertaken for nothing, knowing the man was in the area. The news had reached Murchison before McLennan had shown up. He had been waiting for some time to learn the marshal was close, and had been informed by one of his passing friends, another traveling hunter, about LeRoy being in Clear Springs. The wandering hunter, who frequented the high country, had been in town, spotted LeRoy, and carried the information to him on his way back to his traps. Murchison had carried his personal score to be settled for some long time; and now that it had come, Murchison seized the opportunity. McLennan wanted LeRoy off his trail, and Murchison was the right man for the job.

The second matter was down to Murchison having to live with the fact that his eyesight was deteriorating. He could still get by, but as his vision weakened he was losing his ability to shoot as well as he had for so long. Over the years, Murchison had been well known for his pinpoint shooting, his accuracy over long distances. That skill was fading as he found he was unable to see clearly over those long distances. It concerned him, though he kept the fact to himself. He knew it was partially pride that kept him silent. Murchison refused to let it be known he was losing his edge. The last thing he needed was to have to face people with them knowing his affliction. He needed to stay on top as long as he could. Over the years, he had crossed a number of men who would make it their business to face him down. It was the nature of the beast; and if it became known he was less than at his best, he would be challenged.

With his days as a sharpshooter falling away, he realized he needed to secure some kind of future. His sister had an outfit on the Chug in Wyoming, a nice stretch of land not too far from Laramie. She had run it since her husband died, and with the death of her son she was struggling to keep things going. With the money McLennan had paid him, Murchison would be able to buy in to the spread. However long his eyesight might last, working there would suit him well. It would be a quieter life, but hopefully better than his present one.

When McLennan made his offer, the situation was fortuitous, Murchison thought. It was a word he didn't get to use very often, but right now it fitted well.

Fortuitous.

For Caleb Murchison maybe. But

not for US Marshal Alvin LeRoy. All he would get would be a ticket to hell.

It's coming, lawdog, and there ain't a damn thing you can do to step away from your comeuppance.

He settled in his saddle and eyed the passing clouds, seeing heavy formations coming in from the north. The bulking darkness within the moving mass told him there was a rainstorm on the way, and from its line of travel it would overtake Murchison in an hour or so. It didn't worry him. He knew the best places to shelter if the storm did strike. A man caught in a high-country storm could find himself in danger from sudden flash floods, mudslides, and trees loosened from their roots being washed away. Murchison had experienced everything the mountains could throw at a man and survived. He understood that in this high country, respect for the land was important. Too many men treated it casually and paid the price. Their bones were scattered far and wide. He hadn't lived as long as he had by shrugging his shoulders to the dangers. Those who did deserved whatever calamity descended on them.

Some little time later, he felt the wind rising and saw the distant glow of unnatural light that heralded the coming storm. Tree branches began to bend under the increasing pressure. The first drops of rain came at him, and Murchison unrolled the black slicker he had already pulled from behind his saddle. He shrugged his way into its folds, pulling it down so it spread out over his gear behind his saddle. The gray balked a little as the first rush of rain swept down off the higher ground, but Murchison's firm hand held it steady and it settled quickly.

'Ain't but a rainshower, hoss,' he said. 'We get wet is all.'

He rode slow and steady. The ground underfoot at the best of times could be treacherous to a rider in a hurry. With the rainstorm, the risk was increased. Murchison was heading in the general direction of Clear Springs. If LeRoy had taken it in his mind to continue his search for McLennan, he would be riding *towards* Murchison. If that was the case, they might cross paths. A couple of times Murchison took short-cuts away from the main trail that allowed him to keep it visible. It let him cover a greater distance.

The afternoon faded, and darkness forced Murchison to halt. He chose a spot where a wide overhang of rock offered him some shelter from the persistent rain. He secured the gray near a patch of grass and off-saddled, then hauled his saddle and gear to a dry spot beneath the overhang where he was able to drag off the slicker. There was no chance of finding dry wood for a fire, so he made do with a cold camp. It was far from being the first time Murchison had done so. He had a wedge of cold meat and dry crackers in his saddlebags. That and water from his big canteen comprised his meal. When he had eaten, he took out a thin cigar and lit it. When he finished the cigar, he unrolled his blankets, wrapped them around himself and lay down. He listened to the wind moaning overhead. Heard the rain. He wondered if LeRoy was out in the inclement weather. He didn't dwell on that for too long as he turned on his side to sleep. Come daylight, he was expecting all of his questions would be answered.

★ ★ ★

With Murchison gone, McLennan turned his attention to the second man. He was sitting patiently, watching everything that happened with interest. He didn't say a word until Murchison joined him at his table.

'You seem to be having a busy day,' he said. His voice held the soft trace of his southern background.

His name was Lee Sanford, a slim pale-haired man in his early forties with eyes as cold and empty as a dead fish. He was dressed in a gray suit and a pale striped shirt; and despite some long hours in a swaying coach that had deposited him at Remson's the day before on its wide swing through the area, he looked as fresh as if he'd just stepped out of his tailor's store. His only affectation apart from his fancy clothing was the thin leather gloves covering his slim hands. There was only one time he took off the gloves to expose his hands, and that was when he was working. Sanford's skill lay in his hands. More precisely in his fingertips. His skill was opening safes, working the combinations by touch and his ability to break the sequences in the locks. He had been doing this for a number of years and had an unbroken record. He worked for a percentage of whatever was found in any safe he cracked. Meeting Ty McLennan here at Remson's was no chance encounter. It was all prearranged, explained in the telegrams McLennan had been exchanging with Sanford before he and his partners left Clear Springs after the bank job. From Remson's, the group would carry on over the divide and complete the journey, their destination Junction City. It would be somewhere around the town that Ty McLennan's plan would finally come to fruition.

McLennan held out the bottle of liquor, knowing Sanford would refuse. He always bet against himself that one day Sanford would break his rule and take a drink.

'Ty, you try every time we meet. And every time I say no. So why keep trying?'

'Odds tell me you'll say yes one day.'

'Always the optimist.' Sanford indicated the mug of coffee on the table. 'My indulgence,' he said.

'We're ready to move come morning,' McLennan said. 'Good ride in front of us. Remson have that horse ready for you?'

Sanford nodded. 'I checked it out. Looks sound. I've had plenty of time on my hands waiting for you three to show up.'

'We'll head out first light tomorrow,'

McLennan said.

'Handy I fixed you boys with beds for the night then,' Sanford said.

CLEAR SPRINGS

Rafe Connolly's store — on his sign over the frontage it said 'Connolly's Emporium' — carried most anything a customer could want. When Bodie had stepped inside, he was duly impressed. He figured whatever he might ask for, Connolly would be able to produce it. He crossed to the counter, where the man was serving a young woman. Connolly nodded in recognition, completed his transaction, and confronted the manhunter.

'You leaving, Mister Bodie?'

'Any time now.'

'I don't envy what you have to do.'

'Given a choice, I'd rather be leaning up against a bar with a glass of beer in my hand.'

Connolly reached behind the counter and lifted a filled gunnysack. He laid it in front of Bodie. 'I imagine you have most of the personal things you need, so I took the liberty of including edibles. There's bacon, beans, coffee. Some flour and a couple of cans of peaches. You a drinking man?'

'In moderation.'

'Bottle of whiskey. I put in a roll of bandage and a jar of salve. Just in case things get rough.'

'You'd be surprised at how rough things can get out there.'

'You short on ammunition?'

'Okay for my rifle, but I could do with some .45s.'

Connolly added a couple of boxes, slipping them into the sack. 'Anything else I can do for you?'

'In case I don't have a chance to swing by, just make sure Gunnar's grave is kept tidy.'

'I'll do that with pleasure.'

Bodie picked up the sack and turned to leave, then paused. 'McLennan ain't about to walk free,' he said.

'Never crossed my mind he would.'

Outside, Bodie laid the possibles sack

behind his saddle and secured it after he took the boxes of ammunition and placed them in his saddlebags. He swung into the saddle and rode out of town. Passing the bank, he saw Levi Benjamin framed in the doorway and ignored the man as he passed by. Drawing level with the jail, he watched Alvin LeRoy stepped out, closing the door behind him. LeRoy mounted his own waiting horse and fell in beside Bodie. They left Clear Springs behind and took up the long cold trail left by McLennan and his partners.

Witnesses had told that the trio had ridden out of town in the general direction Bodie and LeRoy were taking. Studying the map of the territory tacked to the wall in the sheriff's office, Bodie had traced a line going in a westerly direction. Anyone going in that direction would be heading for the divide. It would take them clear across the rocky barrier and down into the wider expanse of land on the other side.

'I'd venture they'll stop off at

Malachi Remson's place,' LeRoy had said. 'They left town in a hurry after the robbery, so I'm figuring they'll need to pick up supplies.'

Bodie had agreed. Remson's was the only place where it was possible to buy food this far into the hills. If McLennan was intending to cross the divide, there was nowhere else he could get supplies.

'If they take time to rest up at Remson's, we might gain some leverage,' Bodie said.

He wasn't going to bank on that. But as McLennan and his crew still had the advantage of time and distance, right now it was all Bodie could hope for.

* * *

They rode through the day until the light began to fade. Higher up the rising slopes, a storm had built. Even at a distance, it was plain to see that the dark clouds were dropping rain way ahead of them. Choosing a sheltered place on the fringe of a timbered area,

Bodie built a fire and set to with bacon from the supplies Connolly had contributed. LeRoy produced a blackened coffee pot and filled it with water from one of his large canteens. He added crushed coffee beans and set the pot on the edge of the fire.

'If that storm hits right about where McLennan and his boys are,' LeRoy said, 'it could slow them down. Maybe give us a chance to catch up.'

'Long as it doesn't stretch out down this way.'

'Man can only hope.'

The side of bacon Connolly had provided was large enough to allow Bodie to cut off thick slices. He dropped them into the frying pan he carried in his possibles sack, and with the heat softening the fat that edged the slices, the aroma of cooking bacon soon rose.

'Not French cuisine,' LeRoy said, 'but it'll do.'

He found some reasonably soft biscuits in his own provisions, and when the bacon was cooked through, they were able to make crude but edible sandwiches. Bodie poured brewed coffee into tin cups.

'Word is you partnered up with Jason Brand a couple of times,' LeRoy said. 'How did you get on with him?'

'Good man to have at your side.'

'Frank McCord tells me so.'

'You know McCord?'

LeRoy inclined his head. 'We go back a few years. Being in the law business, our paths have crossed. Man runs his department with a firm hand.'

'Yeah, that's what Brand told me.'

A thin smile curved LeRoy's mouth. 'McCord doesn't give in too easily, and he can be a handful.'

'Brand mentioned that too. Come the day, he isn't a man who takes the easy path himself.'

'Law is still walking a thin line in the wild places,' LeRoy said. 'Calls for a firm hand.' He refilled his coffee. 'You know that better than most. I recall that run-in with Sam Trask down Colton way.'

'We had at it up on the snowline. Came close for a while.'

'You wore a badge yourself a while back?'

Bodie stared off into the distance, ghostly images flitting across his mind as he recalled that time. It hadn't ended well, and he had lost his partner. It was after that Bodie had walked away from the marshal service and took up his bounty hunting. Some years back now. He had moved on ... but the memories still had a bite.

LeRoy sensed he was treading on sensitive ground and said no more on the subject.

* * *

They cleared camp and were in the saddle as daylight broke. Ahead, the sky looked clear as they picked up the pace and headed in the general direction of Remson's place. The day brightened around them, revealing the dense greenery, with the looming presence of the rocky crags as a backdrop. They allowed their horses to pick their route over the uneven ground, the animals stepping cautiously as if they understood the risk of moving too quickly, the slopes rose in a series of undulating swells. Thickets lay in tangled patches, and the timber grew close-ranked. This was unsettled land, with barely an established trail to be seen. Bodie picked out the traces of recent passing, easily missed if you were not a man used to tracking in such terrain. It was part of his business to follow signs, and Bodie had the skill his manhunting depended on. They were only small things at times. Where shod horses had crushed the grass underfoot, leaving imprints that still showed even though they were fading. Snapped twigs on brush that had been pushed through. The telltale signs of horse droppings. Small things, but enough to let Bodie know riders had passed by recently. And the tracks he saw told him there had been three riders — the number who had ridden out of Clear Springs.

The day proved to be pleasant enough. The dark clouds of the previous day had vanished, leaving a clear sky. It was warm enough, though the air at this altitude held a touch of freshness to it that might easily become colder as they climbed higher.

When they passed a clear, tumbling stream that bounded downhill, they paused to let the horses drink while they refreshed themselves and replenished their canteens with the cold water. It allowed the opportunity to stretch their legs and ease the stiffness.

'It's good country,' LeRoy said. 'A man would be hard pressed to find better.'

'That on your mind? Settlin', maybe?'

'Thought passes through from time to time. I ain't fool enough to believe I can do this forever. Man gets to be old.'

Bodie was leaning against his saddle. LeRoy had touched on a subject he considered himself at times. Perhaps more often since meeting Ruby Keoh.

His association with the young woman had forced him to consider his own future. Bodie knew he would reach a time in his life where the rigors of his profession would start to tell on him. He was not vain enough to expect to go on forever. There would come the day when he would need to back off and take up a different kind of life. *Before I come up against someone faster. Someone capable of matching me.* With those thoughts, he was forced to consider what he might do if he did give up his manhunting days. He wasn't cut out to be a clerk in a store, standing behind a counter, or to work behind a bar in a saloon. Riding drag behind a line of cattle didn't hold much appeal either. Dust and flies. Long days on the trail. That was for younger men. A slow smiled curved Bodie's lips. When it came down to it, he wasn't looking at a long list.

Man gets to be old. LeRoy had it right.

'Has to be sense to it all,' LeRoy said.

'They say the mountains were here before man came along to set his footprint. And I'm certain sure they'll still be here after we've all gone. Makes a man consider his own short time.'

Bodie straightened up, swung back into the saddle and waited until LeRoy mounted. 'You set?'

LeRoy nodded and they rode on.

*　*　*

By midday, and Remson's place was still a piece ahead of them. LeRoy figured they might not reach it until after dark. The cool air of earlier had become chill; enough so that they both broke out the thicker coats they carried behind their saddles. They had paused their horses, stepping down to unlimber the coats and shrug their way into them.

Bodie closed his and worked the buttons, his gaze wandering across the timbered stands around them. His action might have been deceptively casual to an observer. His keen gaze was searching, watching for something, anything out of place — like the pale sunlight glancing off something metallic that gave a brief glimmer of reflected light. A distance away, but observable. That shouldn't have been there . . .

Bodie moved without hesitation, turning from his horse and taking long strides, lunging at LeRoy. A startled look crossed the lawman's face as Bodie cannoned into him. The full-on impact knocked LeRoy aside and he stumbled, Bodie following him down. They bumped against LeRoy's horse as they fell, the animal snorting in protest. It jumped aside as the pair slammed to the ground.

The slug hit the dirt just beyond where LeRoy had been standing, sending a spurt of dust and grit into the air.

They were still rolling when the sound of a shot reached them — a solid, heavy shot that had to have come from a large-caliber weapon. The report registered in Bodie's' mind. It was something he had heard before and recalled well. A Sharps rifle, 45–70 caliber. Long-range, and capable of putting a big hole in whatever it hit.

'Stay down,' he said.

LeRoy had heard the shot as well. He moved without a pause, sliding into cover behind a thick tree base, dragging out his handgun.

Bodie had hunkered down behind a slab of rock rising from the ground. It was smaller than he might have chosen, given a chance.

A second shot came, the heavy slug taking a large chunk of timber from the tree LeRoy was using for cover. The third one lifted an even larger piece, and LeRoy felt splinters hit the side of his face, forcing him to draw even further behind the tree. He wasn't in favor of hiding, but necessity overcame pride.

'He's up in those rocks,' Bodie said. 'Sonofabitch has the advantage as long as he stays up there. He can sit all day and wait us out.'

LeRoy glanced at where their horses, spooked by the shots, had moved away and were cropping at a patch of grass. 'And if he has a mind, he can pick off the horses and set us afoot.'

'You had to say that, huh?'

'No point avoiding the fact.' LeRoy felt a trickle of blood slide down his cheek from one of the wood splinters. 'If he keeps pecking away at this tree, I won't have any cover left.'

Bodie was studying the way ahead. The ground rose in a series of humps, well covered with shrubs and timber, that would protect him if he could reach the first section. It would be a tough climb, but not impossible.

'LeRoy, you want to scoot to the other side of that tree and throw a couple shots? Distract our friend so I can get out from behind this damn rock.'

'And do what?'

'I need to reach cover so I can climb that slope.'

LeRoy was silent for a moment. 'You figure to sneak up on him?'

Bodie had his Colt in his hand, checking the action and making certain all six chambers held a load.

'That feller isn't going to wait around all day,' he said. 'That Sharps gives him the advantage. He can stay out of our range and still pick us off. Sooner or later he'll take that lucky shot.'

'Just remind me, Bodie — did you talk me into this, or did I decide it might be a good idea?'

'I'll let you think about that while I take a run up that slope. Now let him catch a look at you to get him to take another shot.'

LeRoy shook his head. 'It's that *take another shot* part that worries me.'

Bodie eased to the far left of his sheltering rock and scanned the way ahead. He would have no more than a few seconds before the rifleman ejected the spent cartridge and loaded a fresh one. Then a few more seconds to pick up his target afresh. Not a long span of time. Bodie was going to need to move damn fast and find himself a fresh place to hide if the shooter decided to switch targets from LeRoy to himself. And as fast as he could move up the slope, it was going to be some time before he maneuvered himself into range for his handgun.

LeRoy slipped out of sight behind the thick tree. When his head and one shoulder were exposed, nothing happened immediately. The marshal held his position for a lot longer than Bodie would have expected, then fired off a pair of shots from his handgun.

Hell, LeRoy, don't push your luck too far.

It could have been an eternity to Bodie before LeRoy ducked back behind the protecting tree. A second later, a 45–70 slug whacked into the trunk, blowing a ragged hole in the wood.

And Bodie moved, mentally counting off time as he dug in his heels and scrambled for his first piece of cover.

*   *   *

Murchison called himself every kind of a fool when he saw LeRoy's partner break cover and head for the slope. The pair of them had drawn him into taking a hasty shot, giving the man his chance. Before he'd been afflicted with his sight problem, he would have been faster acquiring his target and more likely to hit what he was aiming at.

Sonofabitch, Murchison cursed silently.

He reloaded and found himself almost fumbling as he thrust a fresh cartridge into the breech, yanking the action with a hard move.

Ease off, hoss. Don't let them throw you.

Thing was, they were succeeding. Murchison took a long, slow breath and forced himself to steady his nerves. He hadn't been expecting LeRoy to have a partner. That said, he realized his assumption had rebounded on him. It was a fool mistake, and it had created a problem.

Murchison raised the Sharps, swiveling

the barrel in the general direction where the second man had completed his move, allowing himself to be swallowed by the overgrown foliage of the slope. He had to blink his watering eyes as he tried to focus. He couldn't spot him. There was nothing in his sight that might reveal where the man was concealed. Whoever he was, he hid himself well, he had to give him that.

Murchison turned his head, bringing the rifle around, and refocused on the place LeRoy had chosen. There was no movement there. The lawman was staying in cover now that he had given his partner his chance. And as long as he remained there, he was not getting close enough to bring his handgun in range. Murchison smiled. The shots LeRoy had fired off had been nothing more than a distraction. Murchison should have known they couldn't reach him. His response had been a simple reflex action. LeRoy had risked catching a slug just to allow his partner some moving space.

He gave LeRoy credit; not that it made his desire to kill the lawman any less determined. He was set on his course now, and nothing — *not a damned thing* — would alter that. LeRoy owed him a bloody death; and once Caleb Murchison made himself a promise; there was no way to change that.

★　★　★

LeRoy was pretty certain who the shooter was now. There was only one man he knew who handled a Sharps so well, and who worked around the high-divide country.

Caleb Murchison.

The more thought on it, the more convinced he was.

Alvin LeRoy saw Bodie vanish in the greenery that covered the slope. Even though he had a clear view, he lost sight of the manhunter. He knew Bodie would stay out of sight as he climbed towards Murchison's position. There was still the threat from the Sharps. All Murchison needed was a clear shot. The man was known for his skill with the powerful weapon. A hit from one of those 45–70 slugs would put a man down sure as. Even someone as tough as Bodie would drop if one of them hit him.

LeRoy twisted around, searching, and after a while he caught sight of his and Bodie's horses. They were contentedly grazing a couple of hundred yards off from where their riders had left the saddles. LeRoy was thinking about the rifles secure in the saddle boots. The Winchesters could throw lead a great deal further than a handgun. If he could get his hands on one of those weapons, it could even the odds in their favor. LeRoy put away his Colt, slipping the hammer thong into place. He knew what he was considering might place him in the direct line of Murchison's fire, but he was damned if he was going to sit on his butt and let Murchison call the tune.

What the hell. He didn't expect to live forever.

There was risk involved. But LeRoy figured it was reduced a degree because Murchison had *two* targets to consider. If it had been LeRoy on his own, the situation would have been different. With Bodie out there, LeRoy was being offered a chance.

He set himself, hoping Bodie was in a position to see any move he might make, and didn't hesitate. Staying low, he pushed away from his protection and took a scrambled dive for the undergrowth close by. He was aware of the rasp of his own breathing. It sounded loud in his ears, senses raised to acute by the knowledge he was opening himself up to Murchison's close watch. As the brush closed around him, his body growing tense, half-expecting a shot at any second, LeRoy tried to ignore the possibility as he lunged through the tangled undergrowth.

Something whipped through the foliage close by. He felt the passage of the big slug as it chewed and tore at leaves and tendrils. It was like a whisper of death. The sound of the shot followed. Even in his agitated state, LeRoy understood he had been given a few seconds of grace while Murchison reloaded. He increased his speed, ignoring the slap and sting of brush slapping at his clothing. Something was scratching the side of his face. Somewhere along the way, he felt his hat being dragged off his head. He just kept moving, increasing his pace as the thin moment of clear time was whipped away.

Any second now, he thought, *Murchison will have another cartridge in place.*

He would be lifting the rifle. Aiming . . . taking up the first pressure on the pre-trigger before he slid his finger across the main one and dropped the hammer. LeRoy gave a startled yell as something burned across his left shoulder. The bullet graze had not given him any pain when the heavy crack of the shot sounded. LeRoy felt himself tumbling forward into a shallow depression, slamming face down with force enough to drive the breath from his body, and the only thought going through his mind was the hope that the sound of the shot wasn't going to send the horses running again. As LeRoy pushed into a crouch, he began to feel the pain from the bullet burn and the seeping blood running down his back under his shirt.

A slow rising anger drove him forward, feet digging into the soft earth under his boots, his goal to reach the horses, not letting the rifleman win. Behind him he heard the crack of a handgun.

Bodie?

Had to be. LeRoy had almost forgotten about him in his own rush.

Moving at full tilt now, closing his mind to the threat of the rifle, he reached the horses. They were jostling together, near running. LeRoy pushed between them, closing his hand over his rifle and sliding it from the leather sheath. It had never felt as satisfying to feel it in his grasp. As he cleared the bulk of the two horses, LeRoy worked the lever and put the first .44–40 into the breech. He cleared the immediate area, plunging through the under- growth, and swung the Winchester into play, firing off a pair of shots in the general direction of the hidden shooter.

He picked up another pistol shot that was replied to by the rifleman.

LeRoy leaned into the slope, feeling his leg muscles protest, but he kept moving. He had to close the distance and get himself in rifle range.

*　　*　　*

Murchison slid a fresh cartridge in place and snapped the lever back, trying to quell the agitation threatening to take away his calm. He swung the heavy rifle to his shoulder, traversing left and right as he attempted to find a target he could settle on.

LeRoy was still moving upslope, his

Winchester loosing off shots that were getting dangerously close.

The second man had negotiated the uneven slopes with a determination that was unsettling. Whoever he was, he was coming on fast, yet managing to stay within cover, only briefly showing himself and dropping out of sight before Murchison settled long enough to fire. Since his earlier shots, used to distract Murchison while LeRoy moved, the man had not loosed off any more.

Murchison had the feeling he was being hemmed in. A wise move would be for him to retreat. That crossed his mind and was instantly dismissed. Caleb Murchison was not a man to back away from a fight. He never had, and it was too late in his life to become a quitter.

No walking away, hoss. Not from this pair. Let me get at least one on target — hopefully into that sonofabitch LeRoy.

The thought of the marshal dead gave him a boost, and he turned the Sharps downslope and searched for LeRoy. He caught a sliver of blurred movement about where LeRoy should be and edged the rifle forward, anticipating where LeRoy might step next, then held and triggered the Sharps. The recoil kicked the butt against his shoulder, and he saw a flurry of movement in the undergrowth. A feeling of jubilation rose inside him.

Had he hit the man? Put him down?

Murchison reloaded and let the rifle center in on the area. No movement. Murchison looked closer, focusing on the spot. He was sure he could see a dark shape in amongst the greenery. He strained his watery eyes, cursing his inability to focus properly.

* * *

Bodie's tall figure came up from the ground, his Colt held two-handed, and there was no hesitation when he lined up on Murchison. He put a pair of .45 slugs into the man, the impact half-turning Murchison; and he saw LeRoy push upright from where he'd been lying.

The Winchester snapped to his shoulder and cracked sharply, the slug impacting against the rifle in Murchison's hands. The wooden stock splintered as the slug hit, jarring it from Murchison's hands as he stumbled back, his legs going from under him. A second and third shot slammed into his body and he fell on his back, staring in stunned silence as Bodie and LeRoy closed in, weapons still trained on him. As they moved in, their shapes became clearer.

'Caleb Murchison,' LeRoy said.

'You know him?'

'We go back a way. Got a history.'

A mess of blood stained the front of Murchison's buckskin shirt. More was spilling from his mouth. 'Back to when you murdered my sister's boy,' he said, and found it an effort to speak.

'That was no damn murder,' LeRoy said. 'Corey surrendered, then pulled a hideout gun and put a slug in me first. Then I put *him* down.'

Murchison fell to coughing, spitting up gouts of blood from his pain-wracked body. He hunched over, gripping his body. 'I should have . . . '

'Mister, you had your chance and didn't make it,' Bodie said.

Murchison tilted his head and stared at the manhunter, recognition finally dawning. Up close, his vision was clear. 'Bodie. You working with the lawdog now?'

'Only until we catch up with Ty McLennan.'

Murchison made a soft sound of acknowledgement, and something in his expression registered with LeRoy.

'I'll be damned,' he said. 'You took McLennan's money to gun me down. That's how come you knew we were on his trail.'

'I'd have done it for free,' Murchison said. 'But the man paid well, and a body needs to plan ahead.'

'Well, he ain't had his money's worth,' Bodie said.

'We'll tell him when we catch up with him,' LeRoy said.

'I hope he empties his gun in you,'

Murchison said. They were his last words, coughed up as he let his life slip away.

'Feller, he'll need to be a damn sight better than you to do that,' Bodie said.

They found Murchison's horse close by, stripped off its trappings, and set it free. Then they buried Murchison as best they could under a pile of stones, his shattered rifle laid alongside him. LeRoy checked the man's saddlebags. There was little of interest until he found the wad of money. He thumbed through it and showed it to Bodie.

'All a man's life is worth,' Bodie said.

'I'll have it sent to Murchison's sister,' LeRoy said. 'She may as well make use of it, seeing he put his life up for it.'

Bodie reloaded his Colt, LeRoy his rifle. They collected their own horses and moved off in the direction of Remson's place. It was going to be dark by the time they reached it, and they needed food and drink.

They took their time so Bodie could

look at the bullet score in LeRoy's shoulder. It had bled but proved to be little more than a surface gouge. Bodie cleaned it up and laid on some salve LeRoy had in his saddlebags.

'Be sore for a while, but it's clean.'

LeRoy pulled on a fresh shirt and shrugged back into his coat. 'Hell of a bedside manner you got,' he said. 'But thanks anyhow.'

*   *   *

Bodie and LeRoy rode on with the day fading around them, feeling the chill of a wind soughing down off the high peaks. Neither man said very much. They were both wrapped in their own thoughts, aware of what might lie ahead and conscious of their inhospitable surroundings. Here on the divide, the weather had a tendency to change quickly, and seldom for the better.

Bodie's thoughts were centered on his self-imposed commitment to bringing down the killers of his friend,

Gunnar Olsen. His manhunting profession often isolated him from making real friends, and he valued the few he had. Olsen had been one of them — an honest, dedicated man who believed his way of upholding the law was righteous. He had the respect of those who knew him, and for Bodie the man's friendship had been important. That he had died at the hands of a man like Ty McLennan was more than a crime. Bodie was determined to avenge his friend, simple as that. McLennan and his partners, Bell and Krupps, would find the world a smaller place than they believed.

Alvin LeRoy, as much a dedicated man as Olsen had been, held similar feelings where Olsen was concerned. He had known the man, maybe not as well as Bodie, but he had respected his ways. To have died at the hands of craven killers was as bad as it could get. LeRoy respected the law, represented by the US marshal badge he wore, yet right now felt as Bodie did. McLennan and his partners were on their last ride.

Shadows intensified around them. They rode slowly, letting their horses pick their own way. No chances were taken. One fatal step and man and horse might take a killing fall.

They drew rein in a close stand of timber as the first heavy scattering of ice-cold rain struck. Slickers were unfurled and quickly pulled on.

'Remson's has to be close now,' LeRoy said.

'I seen light over yonder,' Bodie said. 'Can't be more'n half a mile.'

'We take a chance? That or we stay here and take whatever the weather throws our way.'

Bodie flashed a brief smile. 'No contest then. I can smell hot coffee already.'

It was an unspoken mutual decision for them to dismount and lead their horses, hunching forward against the slap of the rain. It came at them in fierce sheets, chilling their exposed faces. The horses didn't take to the downpour, occasionally pulling back against the reins. Bodie and LeRoy had to wrap the leathers around their gloved fingers and hold the animals' heads close as they trudged through the storm, which was what it had become. They were forced to ford a stream that was swollen by the runoff tumbling across the slopes. The roiling water reached their knees, soaking into their boots; but as their pants were already sodden, it made little difference.

They were both feeling the cold by the time they reached Remson's. The first thing they did was lead the horses into the stable, where they unsaddled and dried the animals as best they could with blankets hung over the sides of the stalls. They forked in feed and made sure there was water for the pair before they took up their gear and trudged across to the main building.

Warmth reached out to envelop them as they pushed open the door and stepped inside. Remson kept the place well lit with a number of oil lamps, and a fire blazed in the stone hearth. Glancing around, they saw they were the only customers, which suited them both. They pulled off their dripping slickers and hung them from the wooden pegs near the door. It was only when they were done that Remson was able to recognize LeRoy.

'Marshal LeRoy, you chose a hard time to be up here.'

LeRoy managed a tight smile as he laid his gear alongside Bodie's on one of the empty tables, then moved to the bar. 'My work doesn't allow me to choose when I take to the trail.'

'Guess that's true.' Remson took a longer look at Bodie as he bellied up alongside LeRoy. 'Should I know you?' he said.

'Not from here. First visit. Name's Bodie.'

'Heard the name,' Remson said. 'Bounty man?'

'Right now just a feller in need of a mug of hot black coffee.'

'Make that two, Malachi,' LeRoy said.

Remson laid out a pair of mugs, then brought a steaming coffee pot and filled them. 'You fellers ready for a meal?'

LeRoy simply nodded.

'Man has good judgment,' Bodie said.

'Take a seat,' Remson said. 'Help yourselves to fresh coffee when you're ready.'

Bodie said, 'I might never leave if this is the regular service.'

They chose a table near the big pot-bellied wood-burning stove and let the heat chase the chill from their bodies. They were both ready to sit back and relax. They were on their second mugs of coffee when Remson appeared with a pair of loaded plates. He placed them on the table, then went to collect knives and forks. The big platters held steaks and boiled potatoes, beans and rich gravy. A rising wind beyond the walls drove sheeting rain against the building.

'Could be in for a rough night,' Remson said. 'I guess you'll be staying over tonight. Couple of spare rooms in back if'n you want 'em.'

'Sounds like a good idea,' Bodie said. 'Been wet enough for one day.'

Remson seemed hesitant about moving away, and LeRoy picked up on it.

'Ty McLennan was here a day or so back,' Remson said.

'On his own?'

'Bell and Krupps were with him.'

Bodie slice off a wedge of steak, sticking it with his fork. 'They cause any trouble?'

'No. They rested overnight and moved on.'

'They meet up with anyone?'

'Caleb Murchison was here when they showed up. McLennan had a pow-wow with him right over there. Like they were old friends, all secretive and close-mouthed. Then Murchison just up and leaves, like he had somewhere to go in a hurry.'

'He had somewhere to go,' Bodie said. 'Like trying to blow off our heads with that Sharps he carried.'

'He tried to kill you?'

'*Tried* being the operative word,' LeRoy said. 'Murchison went down fighting. Give him that.'

Remson stared between them. 'You saying he come looking for you?'

'No other way of looking at it,' Bodie said. 'And he had a sizable roll of cash in his poke.'

'Have to say old Caleb was always ready to sell his gun. I heard the stories about him over the years. He was always ready to step over the line. Never had any problems with him myself. You figure he made a deal with Murchison?'

'McLennan and his boys hit the bank in Clear Springs and took off in this direction,' LeRoy said. 'They killed Gunnar Olsen when he got in their way.'

'Olsen?' Remson was genuinely shocked by the news. 'Gunnar was a fine man.'

'Too good to be cut down by the likes of McLennan,' Bodie said.

'You knew him?'

Bodie met his stare. 'He was a friend.'

'You pick up any talk while McLennan was here?' LeRoy asked.

'Not a deal. Him and his boys stayed pretty close. Only thing I did get was the name of the feller they joined up with.'

'They met someone here?' LeRoy said.

'Feller showed up while before they rode in. Dropped off the stage that passes by every week. Took a room and bought a horse from me. Just sat around quiet like. Wasn't the type for conversation. Stared out the window most of the time. Odd feller. He rode out with them when they left. McLennan called him Sanford . . . '

LeRoy turned in his chair. 'Lee Sanford?'

'Never heard his first name. Just Sanford. He someone you know?'

'Tell me what he looked like.'

'Skinny feller. Light blond hair. Dressed fine. Gray suit. Striped shirt. Real neat feller. He had the coldest eyes I ever saw this side of a dead fish. Gave

96

a man a funny feel when he looked at you.'

'Anything else that caught your attention?'

Remson said, 'His hands . . . '

'Covered by black gloves he never took off?'

'Yeah. Wore them all the time. Even when he was eating. Never saw the like before.'

'Sounds like you know him,' Bodie said.

'Damn right I do. Lee Sanford is the best safe cracker I ever came across. He can open any combination lock made. Law has been after him for years. He's always just out of reach. Sharp hombre. Sharp enough to keep out of jail.'

'Gloves?' Bodie said.

'Barely ever takes them off. His trademark, I'd say. Protection for his fingers. That's where his skill lies, in his fingertips. He damages them and his safe-cracking days are over.'

'McLennan must have something big to go after if he needs someone like this

Sanford,' Bodie said.

'That's what worries me.'

'Clear Springs' bank,' Bodie said. 'McLennan took over $20,000. Could be he's using that to bankroll whatever he's got planned for next time.'

'That's what I've been thinking. If it's true, it must be really big.'

If Ty McLennan was planning something spectacular, Bodie and LeRoy would need to catch up with him. The problem was, they only had a general impression of which direction to head in, and no clear knowledge what target he had in mind. That wasn't going to be helpful.

* * *

Leaving Remson's, the outlaws picked up the trail that would take them across the divide and in turn down the opposite western slopes. The final stretch took them over the high ridges and through rugged passes and timbered terrain that hit them with bitter winds and cold rain. It was harsh weather under darkened cloud-heavy skies.

Of them all, it was Krupps who complained most. He was cold. He was wet. Tired of the long ride. Sick of . . .

'He ever stop grumbling?' Sanford said, riding alongside McLennan.

'Not often.'

'A man could get really tired of listening to it.'

'Lee, you only been with us a day.'

'So what does that tell you?'

'Roy can be a pain in the butt. He's also one of the fastest with a gun I ever knew. And he always hits what he aims at. Comforting to know in my line of work.'

Sanford considered that. Comfort or not, he figured, having to listen to Krupps' whining was a high price to pay. He hunched deeper into the long waterproof coat he wore, his sodden hat dripping water down the back of his neck, and hoped that whatever McLennan had planned paid off well. It would need to after riding through this cold, wet weather across the mountain slopes, with Roy Krupps complaining in his ear and an uncomfortable saddle chafing at his rear end.

'Ty, we goin' to find a dry place to sit out tonight?' Krupps said. 'You know where we are?'

'I know exactly, son, so quit grumbling.'

'Day he quits jawin',' Bell said, 'we'll know he's done gone and died on us.'

'Better be plenty of greenbacks to come after all this,' Krupps said.

McLennan turned in his saddle, a thin smile on his rain-splashed face. 'Son, you'll have enough to bury yourself under.'

The words etched themselves in Lee Sanford's mind. Ty McLennan was not given to uttering casual remarks. So if he mentioned a large payoff, then Sanford took it to mean what he said. He assessed what he knew. That he had been brought into the deal because of his skill at opening safes — and this one sounded as if it was a big one, in size and holding capacity.

Now what did McLennan have planned? And where?

Sanford knew the man had a fertile imagination, though he often let himself down by going for small thefts, like the one at Clear Springs. Though it now appeared there had been good reason. McLennan had needed a stake that would go to finance the operation they were riding towards. Money in his possession to pay for the next score. A much larger deal — which he had not yet revealed, because he needed to keep his cards close before he showed his hand.

The questions floating around inside Sanford's mind were enough to keep him occupied to the point of forgetting his physical discomfort. He satisfied himself that he would find out when McLennan decided to tell them his plan and how he intended to carry it out.

Sanford found his curiosity piqued.

Now the notion existed, he was finding it hard to push to the back of his mind. As he rode alongside McLennan and caught his eye, Sanford found the man had a quirky expression on his face.

'You too, Lee? Krupps got you itching to know what's up ahead?'

'Can't blame a man for craving an answer.'

'No problem with that,' McLennan said. 'Just don't ride me too hard until I'm ready to give it up.'

McLennan urged his horse forward, leaving Sanford even more curious, and not a little left out. He quelled the feeling. No point getting all worked up over something he would learn about in a short enough time.

An hour later, a solidly built cabin came into view, and McLennan turned his horse towards it. Smoke drifted from the stone chimney. Three unsaddled horses stood beneath a lean-to at the side of the cabin. McLennan drew rein outside the structure.

'Hey in there,' he said.

After a minute, the door opened and a massive figure emerged, staring up at McLennan. The man was clad in thick clothing that added to his natural bulk.

'Took your damn time getting here,' he said.

'Good to see you too, Mackie,' McLennan said as he dismounted, loosening his saddlebags and draping them across his shoulder. 'Roy, see to the horses.'

'Why me?'

'Just do it, huh?'

Muttering to himself, Krupps led the horses to the lean-to, while the others followed the man called Mackie into the cabin.

*   *   *

The interior was heavy with heat from a stone-built fireplace. It was furnished with basic needs that included a scarred wooden table and benches and a couple of bunks. A pair of large oil lamps provided smoky illumination.

McLennan recognized the two other

men seated at the table. 'Telford, Congrave,' he said by way of greeting.

Darren Congrave, a spare man in his forties, nodded. He was hunched over the table, a mug of coffee in his hands. His thick mustache, in need of a trim, was speckled with gray, as was his unruly dark hair. He wore steel-rimmed spectacles, his pale eye large behind the thick lenses.

'We got to thinking you might not make it.'

'Pass on this deal?' McLennan said. 'No chance of that.'

He peeled off his outer clothing and crossed to stand in front of the fire, rubbing his hands together. There was a large coffee pot on the side and he picked up a tin cup, pouring himself a drink.

Seeing this, Bell and Sanford helped themselves, and they clustered around the fire. Krupps came in from seeing to the horses, closing the door behind him. He joined the others and poured himself a drink.

'So, you have any problems?' Telford said.

McLennan smiled. 'I got your money, if that's what you're worried about.'

'Well, hell, I ain't in this for the fun of it,' Telford said. A lean pockmarked man in his thirties, his eyes sharp and searching, he gave the impression of restlessness as he stared across at McLennan. His gaze was challenging.

'You want your money now?' McLennan said.

Telford nodded, his movements sharp. He was almost bald. What hair that remained brushed across his skull. 'If you don't mind.'

McLennan opened one of the saddlebag pouches and drew out a package wrapped in old newspaper. He tossed it across the table and it landed close to Telford's hands. He snatched it up and tore it open, staring at the thick bundle of banknotes.

'All there,' McLennan said. 'What I promised. But you can count it if it suits.'

Telford did just that, his fingers flicking through the wad of money.

Krupps gave a throaty laugh. 'You'd think he didn't trust you.'

McLennan waited until Telford completed his count. 'What have you got to tell me?' he said.

Telford said, 'You think you've given me enough to pay for the information?'

A hard silence descended. McLennan didn't say a word; just raised his head and caught Krupps' eye. Krupps, standing to the side, reached for the knife sheathed in his belt. When he moved, it was faster than anyone could have anticipated. The steel of the blade glittered as Krupps slid behind Telford. He clamped a hand over Telford's forehead and yanked his head back. The keen edge of the cold steel pressed against Telford's taut flesh. He let out a shrill cry.

'I wouldn't do too much wriggling around,' Krupps said. 'Liable to cut your own throat. This blade is sharp.'

'I'm disappointed in you, Cleve,'

McLennan said. He stood over Telford. 'Now I hate a man who reneges on a deal. Understand me? Your part of the deal was to give me important information. If you don't, and it ends this deal, I'll walk away but you will be dead. Believe that, because if I get caught, they can only hang me once. So I got nothing to lose. Your choice.'

Telford's face registered the fear overwhelming him. He had made a bad mistake trying to coerce more money from McLennan. He could feel the razor edge of the knife against his flesh, blood seeping from the slight cut it had made.

'I'll tell,' he said, deciding his attempted ploy had failed miserably and McLennan had called his bluff. So he gave up the information McLennan needed. Sweat beaded his face as he spoke, aware of the recklessness he had exhibited.

'That all of it?' Bell said.

Telford almost nodded but thought better of it. He whispered the acknowledgment, 'Yes. Everything.'

McLennan glanced at the others, his

expression neutral. He drank coffee. Let the silence drag on. 'In a deal like this, we have to trust each other. Has to be that way all down the line,' he said. 'Ain't that so?'

Heads nodded in agreement.

'See, Cleve, we can't trust you now, any of us. And I got to look out for the boys here.'

McLennan nodded briefly at Krupps, who offered a slight smirk. He moved the knife and cut Telford's throat wide open, left to right, in a powerful motion. Blood was flushed from the severed flesh, spilling down Telford's front. He squirmed in a futile attempt to stay alive.

McLennan picked up the wad of money from the table and threw it to Mackie. 'You and Congrave can split that. Figure it a bonus.'

The sound of Telford's heels jerking against the floor came and went as his body slid from the chair.

'Telford made his mistake and paid for it,' McLennan said. 'I'll back any man who plays square with me. All the way down the line. He tried to break his word. Figured he could take me for a damn fool. He got it wrong.'

'I think we all got the message,' Congrave said.

'Roy, move him outside,' McLennan said. 'We got things to talk over.'

'Damn right we do,' Krupps said. 'Just what the hell is going on, Ty? You done told us nothin' about this deal.'

'Move Telford and I'll fill you in.'

McLennan refilled his coffee and waited until Krupps had dragged Telford's body out of the cabin and returned, his face showing his annoyance at being kept in the dark.

'Well?' Krupps said.

'I kept quiet because I didn't want to risk anyone figuring out what we're going to do.'

'Even us?' Bell said.

'No offense meant, Marty. There's too much riding on this to have something slip out, even accidental. A loose word in the wrong place could have someone getting curious. Suspicious. I been working on this a while.'

'So what the hell was Clear Springs all about?' Krupps said. 'Small-town bank. Why bother?'

Getting over the previous slight, Bell said, 'Stake money. Right? To pay off the likes of Telford and the others. That it, Ty?'

'That's it. Like I said, we got a lot hanging on this. Can't afford anything spoiling our shot.'

'That why you wanted LeRoy dealt with?' Krupps said.

'Meeting Murchison at Renfrew's was favorable. Offered a chance to have that lawman taken off our backs.'

'You reckon it worked?' Bell said.

McLennan shrugged. 'We'll know one way or the other.'

'LeRoy ain't no damn tenderfoot,' Krupps said.

'Mebbe so,' McLennan said. 'But Murchison didn't just come down the pike.'

From his saddlebags he drew out two

more wrapped bundles and handed them to Mackie and Congrave. They took the money and the late Sanford's stack, dividing it between them.

'Happy, boys?' McLennan said.

'No complaints here,' Congrave said.

Mackie smiled as he slid his money and the bonus into his coat pocket.

'Now that we're all a happy family again,' Krupps said, 'how about telling us what all this is for, Ty? Times, dates Telford told you? You goin' to tell us?'

'Simple enough,' McLennan said. 'We have a train to catch near Junction City. It's going to be hauling enough money to keep us all in clover for the rest of our lives . . . *and were going to steal it.*'

* * *

'Man who stays as quiet as you, LeRoy, must have something heavy on his mind,' Bodie said.

They had been riding for hours, and LeRoy had barely spoken. Bodie was no big talker himself at times, but the silence between them had finally reached its limit, and the manhunter felt the need to break it.

'Ty McLennan hasn't gone to all this trouble for pocket change. Man is aiming high this time. I reckon he's setting up his biggest robbery. Maybe his last before he retires. Clear Springs for stake money. Lee Sanford because whatever McLennan is going for needs the best help available.'

'Worth considering,' Bodie said. 'McLennan's last stand. Could be.'

'He paid Caleb Murchison to get me off his back trail.'

'He's determined to have a clear field,' Bodie said. 'Man has something important on his mind.'

They found a sheltered spot beneath a high rock formation and made camp beneath a deep overhang of weathered stone. While LeRoy saw to the horses, Bodie took a small hand-axe from his possibles bag and went in search of fuel for a fire. Darkness was fast falling by the time they had a fire burning and water heating for coffee. Shadows lengthened and the night closed in around them. Rain continued to fall.

'You want beans — or beans?' Bodie said. 'There's still a wedge of bacon, but I'm less inclined to go to the trouble of cooking it.'

LeRoy managed a grin. 'I'll go for the second offering.'

'Beans it is.'

Each man produced a tin plate and mug from his gear and a spoon to eat with. It was simple enough fare that would at least help to fill their stomachs. Existence on the trail could become bland where food was concerned, unless a man was able to get lucky and shoot himself a deer or maybe catch fish from a fast-flowing stream. There was little choice otherwise, and a man became accustomed to primitive eating. The reward was that when he reached a regular town, he might find himself faced with a choice of restaurants. Then he could go in for rich steak with potatoes and greens.

Right now, Bodie and LeRoy pushed those thoughts out of their minds as they dined on hot beans washed down with strong coffee. Bodie produced one of the cans of peaches from his supplies. He opened it and they shared the fruit. After they had eaten, LeRoy took a couple of tolerable cigars, and they sat at their meager fire and made sure they emptied the coffee pot before settling down for the night.

Each was going over the thoughts they harbored. LeRoy wondered what they would find when — not if — they caught up to McLennan and his bunch. He was becoming increasingly curious as to what the man was planning . . . and where and when.

Slowly savoring the cigar, Bodie's main thought was centered on Ty McLennan. Sure, he was siding with the marshal on this. But strong in his thoughts was his need to settle matters for his friend. Gunnar Olsen had been worth a hundred Ty McLennans. It had been a loss to everyone who knew the lawman. Clear Springs would not find as good a man as Gunnar. Not ever. Bodie understood that putting McLennan down would not bring his friend back, but even so, his obligation to Gunnar Olsen would not be complete until the man who killed him paid. If it took spilled blood to do it, Bodie had no qualms about pulling the trigger.

He finished his smoke, pulled his slicker over his blankets, and slept.

* * *

'Mackie here is ex-army. He knows weapons and he's got his hands on a special gun that will increase our odds.'

'Ex-army, you say?' Krupps echoed. He glanced across at Mackie.

'Eight years,' Mackie said. 'Master sergeant in charge of ordnance.'

'Until . . . ?'

Mackie managed a wide grin. 'They figured they could do without me when some weapons went missing. Couldn't definitely prove it was down to me, but we came to a parting of the ways after that.'

'Because?' Bell said.

'Most likely because I'd been diverting gun acquisitions over the border and they weren't smart enough to catch me with my hands full.'

'Lucky you didn't get a firing squad.'

'They kicked me out anyhow. Hell, I'd had enough of army life,' Mackie said. 'That was when McLennan made me an offer.'

'You know McLennan?'

'Me and Ty go back a way.'

'So what's this special piece of artillery you got?' Krupps said. 'Ain't a damn cannon?'

'Let's say the army isn't as smart as it believes. I had connections higher up. I used 'em to cover me. You think I was goin' to walk away with empty hands?'

'So you going to let us in on this damn gun?' Bell said.

Mackie glanced at McLennan. He gave a nod. 'You heard of a Gatling gun?'

116

'I heard,' Bell said, 'but I ain't ever see one.'

'Ain't that some fancy repeating weapon?' Krupps said. 'Has a mess of barrels and a big load. Saw a drawing in a pictorial one time.'

'Not advised to stand in front of it, 'less you got no future,' Mackie said.

'Gatling will cut you into little chunks,' McLennan said. 'Take my word. It's a hell of a weapon.'

'I seen one in action,' Congrave said, 'being demonstrated for the military. They fired on a cow carcass.' He gave a smirk. 'Cut that beef into shreds.'

'How came you to be there?' Bell said.

'I was doin' some demonstrating myself.'

'Darren here is our dynamite man,' McLennan said. 'He blows things up.'

Bell held up a hand. 'Now let's figure this out. We got a feller who opens safes. A gunsmith and a dynamite man. Christ, Ty, ain't it time you sat down and explained just what in hell you got planned?'

117

'Set easy, boys. It ain't as hard as you're figuring.'

'So easy you forgot to tell us,' Krupps said, his tone still aggrieved.

McLennan let go an exasperated sigh. 'Roy, we got to get beyond this. Last while I had a lot of arranging to do. While I was playing deputy in Clear Springs, I had to keep sending telegrams to these boys. Keep 'em up to date with things. You figure how hard it was with that dumb lawman around town. I tell you, son, it was hard work. Had to write messages no one could understand 'cept Lee. He had to keep in touch with the others so we could all meet up here and fix the final dates.'

'Dates for what?' Krupps said.

'A special shipment. That was what Telford was here for, to pass along final dates and times. For the train that's going to be carrying our money. That sorry sonofabitch was in for a cut, same as everyone here, on top of what I paid to 'em.'

'Well hell, Telford sure enough got his

cut,' Krupps said.

'Better be the last time you make that crack,' Bell said. He turned back to McLennan. 'How much?'

'Enough so you'll all get enough dollars in your hands to last until you're old men.'

'Damn, don't you be foolin' with me,' Krupps said.

'That train will be carrying a fortune in cash. That kind of money doesn't call for us fooling around.'

'That will go for the folk transporting it as well,' Bell said.

'That's why we got Mackie along. Him and his Gatling gun.'

'What about Congrave?'

'Train runs on steel rails,' Congrave said. 'Blow the rails she ain't got nowhere to go, especially if the ones behind are blown as well.'

Bell tool a moment to consider. 'Looks as if you got this all worked out, Ty.'

'Planning does it ever' time.'

'What we goin' to be doing in the middle of all this?'

'Watching over Lee once we get him inside the money car and he goes to work on the combination. He'll need time. No way that part of the business can be hurried.'

'Safe will be a big one. Made by the Mosler Safe and Lock Company of Cincinnati. One of the best safes there is,' Sanford said.

'What if you *can't* get in?'

Sanford smiled patiently. 'Way that safe is constructed, the only way in is through the open door. Even Darren couldn't open it with his dynamite. No offense, Darren.'

Congrave said, 'None taken. I heard about those Mosler safes. All dynamite would do is scorch the paint. They made them with the best steel around. Mebbe three, four inches thick. Dynamite blast would just bounce off. Door hinges are inside. Door sits flush against the frame. Like Lee says, the only way in is by working the combination.'

'Whole safe is bolted down through the metal base of the car. Even if you could cut it free, it's too heavy to move,' McLennan said.

'And you can open it?' Krupps said.

'Yes.'

'Easy to say,' Bell said. 'I ain't doubting you, but it sounds like it could be a hell of a job.'

'You expecting it to come easy?' McLennan said.

Krupps sniggered. 'That'd be nice.'

'Listen up,' McLennan said. 'Train we're after comes through day after tomorrow. After it leaves Junction City, it travels through a handy ravine. Handy for us. That's where we hit it. Darren will plant his dynamite to take up the track ahead. Soon as the train stops, Darren blows the track behind. That means we have the train caught in the middle. Telford's information has a seven-man escort on the train. Two in the car holding the safe, along with a couple of railroad employees. The other five guards will be in the carriage between the loco and the money car. Mackie will have his Gatling already set up overlooking the spot. That gun will keep the guards covered. Any of them who poke their heads out will get a burst of Gatling fire. Mackie's job is to keep them off our backs. Same with the fellers in the money car. Soon as we have that done, Lee goes to work.'

'How far will the train be from Junction City when it reaches the ravine?' Bell said.

'Far enough so they won't hear the dynamite,' McLennan said.

'Let's hope so.' Krupps made no attempt to hide his concern.

Bell poured himself fresh coffee. He confronted McLennan. 'Ty, we going to pull this off free and clear?'

'No reason why not,' McLennan said. 'Let's be honest, Marty. Ain't never been a job that doesn't have *some* risk. You should know that much as I do. Comes down to whether a man has the guts to try.'

'Guess so. I have to say I could do with a big win. Man gets to an age he's ready to walk away and make a fresh start. If this deal pays the big bucks, I reckon I can play my hand and take my chance.'

'We do this right, boys, we take ourselves a big reward. Hell yes, there's a risk, but we're the ones to take it. Our final job with the biggest reward we'll ever get. We ride out come day's end. Make a wide loop around Junction City and get set up in plenty of time. When that money train shows up, we go to work.'

* * *

'Nearest town of any note is Junction City,' LeRoy said. 'Could be where they're heading.'

'Anything special there?'

'They call it Junction City because it's a spot where railroad tracks come together. Feeder lines for four compass points come together there.' LeRoy fell silent as a thought entered his head.

'Don't go holding out on me now,' Bodie said.

'A while back I heard talk about a

plan to issue new bank notes to replace worn-out ones. There was going to be a gather of old currency from several major banks. The old notes were to be hauled to a chosen place and all secured to be transported by rail to a federal center for burning. New bank notes would be passed out in exchange to all the banks involved.'

'What kind of money are we talking about here?'

'I'd hate to be the feller who had to count it. Old bank notes. No way of making a list of the numbers. Anyone who got hold of that haul would be set for life. Hell, for two lifetimes. Could be talking about close to a million dollars, maybe more.'

'And Junction City could be the rendezvous point where all this money gets loaded onto one train?'

'I'm making a wild guess here about Junction City and Ty McLennan,' LeRoy said.

'Guess or not,' Bodie said, 'McLennan's bunch. This feller Sanford. Clever at opening safes. I'd bet my money on that theory, LeRoy.'

'Only one I have.'

'I've ridden out on thinner than that.'

*   *   *

Close on midday, after a hard ride, they came across the isolated cabin and saw the overlapping signs left by a number of horses. The rain had petered out by then, and though the ground was still soft, there were still faint signs showing; enough to prove recent activity around the cabin.

With guns drawn, they approached the place. Inside, they recognized signs of recent activity. Fresh ash in the fireplace. A pot holding cold coffee that still smelled recent. Scraps of food. And a dark stain on the floor.

'Blood?' LeRoy said.

Bodie rubbed the stain and his fingers came up red. He stood and walked out of the cabin, following the faint scuff marks he had spotted on the cabin floor. They were showing faintly in the soft earth, but Bodie picked up on them. He followed them into a tangle of bushes off to the side.

'LeRoy.'

When the lawman appeared, Bodie showed him the body part concealed in the undergrowth. When he turned the man over, they were able to see the crusted gash in his throat.

LeRoy crouched beside the body and went through the man's coat. He came out with a badge in a leather holder and held it up for Bodie. 'Railroad superintendent,' he said. He stood, turning the badge over in his fingers. 'This man would have known about train schedules. Arrivals and departures.'

'Useful if you want to be around when a certain train shows up.'

'The pieces are starting to fit together. But why kill him?'

Bodie shrugged. 'Double-cross? He delivered his information, so he wasn't any more use to them?'

'Or he tried to force more money for

the information. They called his bluff, got what they wanted, and decided he'd stepped over the line.'

'Whichever it was, he went and missed the train.'

LeRoy checked the sky. 'It's going to be dark in a couple of hours. We need to make up some time. Maybe have to do some night riding. You happy about that, Bodie?'

'Not really, but I don't see we have a choice. Should be a good moon tonight. If we ride steady, there's no reason why we shouldn't reach Junction City in one piece.'

'I can telegraph my people and tell them what we suspect. With luck, we might have that train alerted.'

They took time to let their horses rest from the earlier long ride. Bodie got a fire going and they brewed some fresh coffee. He even fried up what was left of their bacon. It was no gourmet meal, but it would see them through the night. The only good thing was the weather easing off. If the rain stayed away, it would offer them an easier ride to Junction City.

'If McLennan and his bunch pull this robbery off and get clear, they'll be rich men,' LeRoy said. 'Way I see it, they'll scatter and each man go his own way.'

Bodie stared down into his coffee mug, thinking that McLennan was not going to disappear free and clear. The manhunter had his way mapped out in his mind: one-way trail that would lead him to McLennan. He had no intention of allowing the man to go unpunished.

★   ★   ★

The outlaws rode in close on eight in the evening. Junction City was still open for business in the part of town they were interested in. They located the livery and stabled their horses. Walking back along the main street, they saw that a number of saloons were still plying for business. They made their way inside one called The Lucky Hand, which was still open but not too busy.

'No trouble, boys,' McLennan said. 'Couple of beers and some food. After that, we can go take a look at Mackie's lady friend.'

'Huh?' Krupps said.

They picked an empty table and sat.

'Miss Gatling,' Bell said.

Realization dawned, and Krupps managed a grin.

'See?' Mackie said. 'He ain't so dumb.'

Krupps had turned to beckon the bartender across, so he missed the comment. 'You still cooking?' he said.

When the bartender said yes, food and drink were ordered. The beers came first, providing some comfort for dry throats. By the time the food arrived — thick steaks with fried beans and potatoes — they were starting to relax.

Except for Roy Krupps. His restless attitude became noticeable, especially to Bell. He knew his partner too well. Krupps wanted more than just a beer. He craved whiskey. Bell recognized the signs and didn't like them. When Krupps needed his whiskey, he let every other thought slip away, and when he took his whiskey he often lost control. Roy Krupps with whiskey blood could turn bad. Out on the trail with enough to occupy him damped down his urge. Now, in a saloon, where the very air held the taint of liquor, Krupps was starting to become restless. The signs were there.

Krupps ignored his meal and banged his fork on the table, staring around until he spied the bottles lined up behind the bar. 'Want a drink,' he said.

McLennan, his fork halfway to his mouth, said, 'Roy, you got a drink.'

Krupps pushed the beer glass across the table, his cheeks darkening with anger. 'That? That ain't a damn drink. It's like drinkin' cat piss. Okay for you ladies. I want a real drink. Whiskey.'

Bell reached out to touch Krupps' arm, but his partner snatched it away.

'It's okay,' McLennan said. 'Leave him be, Marty. You go and get your whiskey, Roy.'

'See?' Krupps said. 'Bossman knows what I want.' He pushed to his feet and headed for the bar. Bell glanced at McLennan.

'We can't afford a scene,' McLennan said. 'Last thing we need is to draw attention to ourselves and get the local law involved. We're going to have to hope Roy doesn't go too far.'

'You mean like he didn't go too far in Creel?'

'What happened in Creel?' Sanford said.

'Roy got raving drunk, swiggin' whiskey straight out the bottle. Started in on wrecking the saloon. Put a man down by smashing a bottle over his head. Took on the town marshal and his deputies. Three of 'em.' Bell nodded at McLennan. 'You remember that, Ty?'

'Not likely to ever forget. I had to do some fast talking and pay up even faster to get us out of there.'

'If he's such a risk . . . ' Sanford said.

'Why do we stick with him? He's one of us,' Bell said. 'You side with a man, you do it through thick and thin. It's what you do. Ain't that so, Ty?'

'If you can't do that, what are you?' McLennan said. 'Hell, Roy can be a pain in the butt, but come the day he'll always be ready to stand at your side. Can't ask for more.'

'See him draw that pistol and you'll know why he's one of the best,' Bell said. 'He makes it look easy, and he's one the straightest shooters I ever seen.'

'Ty, he could still be a risk,' Sanford said.

McLennan had to accept that. He watched as Krupps downed a third shot, showing the vacuous smile that said he was loosening up. 'Marty,' he said.

Bell took a look at his partner at the bar, shaking his head. He understood what was unsettling McLennan. He knew what it could mean. Krupps. Whiskey. Trouble . . .

He slid his chair back and stood, then turned and crossed to stand beside Krupps.

'Hey, partner, you coming to keep me company?' Krupps said, reaching for his third whiskey.

Bell put his hand on Krupps' shoulder. 'Ease off, partner,' he said. 'We got to keep clear heads now. Busy time coming up.'

There was a trace of irritation in Krupps' voice. He edged away from Bell. 'Don't you worry about ol' Roy Krupps, now. I can handle it.' He banged his fist on the bar. 'Hey, top me up.' He threw coins on the bar and reached for the freshly filled glass.

Bell glanced back at McLennan, a silent question as to what he should do with Krupps. McLennan jerked his head in the direction of the door.

Take him outside. Help him walk it off.

'Let's go find somewhere else to drink,' Bell said. 'Too damn quiet in here for me. Leave the ladies to their beers.'

Krupps looked at him, then took a glance in the mirror over the bar where

133

he could see McLennan and the others.

'Yeah. You got that right, partner. We need somewhere with a livelier crowd.'

With Bell close at his side, Krupps walked out of the saloon, slightly unsteady.

McLennan breathed easier. When Krupps took on his whiskey mood, Bell was the only one who could calm him. He settled in his chair and concentrated on eating, hoping that Marty Bell could work his touch on Krupps before anything untoward happened.

He didn't know it then, but it was a forlorn hope that was going to have unforeseen repercussions.

* * *

Bodie and LeRoy trailed into Junction City mid-morning. Though the sky was clear, the morning was chill, with a cool breeze tugging at their clothing. They were admittedly weary after the long saddle hours. Even their horses were played out, and like their riders were ready for rest and food. LeRoy asked directions for a livery, and they found it at the far end of the surprisingly long street. Junction City gave the appearance of being a busy town. Behind the buildings on their left lay the rail yard, and they were able to pick up the sound of idling locomotives. A pall of smoke drifted up from the yard and the clank of restless couplings could be heard.

The livery was a large cared-for construction. As they dismounted, easing the aches from their limbs, a man emerged from the wide-open doors. He looked to be in his late forties, thin and with a thatch of straw-colored hair. He wore well-used overalls over a gray shirt. He took a long look at horses and riders.

'Long ride?' he said.

'Long enough,' Bodie said. 'You got room for a couple of wore-out horses?'

'Can oblige. Where you fellers come from?'

'Beyond the divide,' LeRoy said, taking his saddlebags and rifle.

'Daresay you rode through some bad weather.'

'You got that right,' Bodie said. 'Be obliged if you gave these horses the best in the house. Rub-down. Plenty of grub and rest.'

'How long for?'

'Can't rightly say yet,' LeRoy said.

Moving around his horse, his coat opened, showing the badge pinned to his vest. The liveryman took note. 'You fellers on business here?'

'Could be if the fellers we're looking for stopped over,' Bodie said. 'LeRoy's a US marshal, so I'm not asking for the fun of it.'

'Well I see most folk who ride in if they're staying around. My name's Orrin Mayberry, by the way.' He glanced at Bodie. 'You a lawman as well?'

'In a manner of speaking. Bodie.'

'Bounty man, right?'

'It's nice to be right. So how about a bunch who rode in recently? They would've come in over the divide.

136

Maybe five of them. Could be more,' Bodie said.

Mayberry considered the question. He glanced back over his shoulder. 'Six riders come in last night. They looked same as you fellers, like they'd had a long ride, and they come in by the same trail you did. Put up their horses and took off up into town.'

'You didn't see just where they went?' LeRoy said.

'Uh-huh. Tell the truth, I was busy with their horses.'

'Those horses still here?'

'Yeah. They haven't been back for 'em yet.' Mayberry stared across at LeRoy. 'They wanted men?'

LeRoy nodded. 'Mister Mayberry, if they do show up, don't say anything that might warn them. They're a rough bunch. If you do see them, let us know. Quietly. Understand?'

'Yessir, Marshal.'

'Tell me where the town marshal has his office and the telegraph.'

Bodie and LeRoy made their way to the marshal's office.

The marshal was around forty, a spare man with graying hair and a no-nonsense look about him. He was bent over paperwork as Bodie and Leroy walked in, and continued writing until he reached the end of his scribing. He glanced up and eyed the two men. His eyes settled on LeRoy's badge and he sat back, hands placed flat on the scarred surface of his desk.

'This an official visit, Marshal?'

LeRoy managed a thin smile. 'In my line of work, is there any other kind?'

'Just when I was figuring things were getting nice and quiet. So what can I do for you, Marshal . . . ?'

'LeRoy. Alvin Leroy. This is Bodie.'

'Interesting. I heard of you, Bodie, but not Mister LeRoy. I'm Jim Conagher.' He leaned forward and shook hands, then motioned them into wooden chairs. 'You fellers want coffee? Have to tell you I make it hot and real strong.'

The coffee, in thick china mugs, was exactly as Conagher promised. He returned to his own seat. 'Now what's this all about?'

Conagher was a good listener. He didn't say a word until LeRoy had given him the story. Considering what he had heard, he nodded his head slowly, then turned to Bodie. 'There a bounty on these fellers?'

'If there is, I ain't interested. It's a personal thing. Gunnar Olsen was a friend. Known him a long time. He was a good lawman. Didn't deserve to die the way he did.'

'You'll get no arguments on that from me. I heard about him. Hell, a lawman who went unarmed. Had to be something special to do that.'

'He was.'

'Marshal, I need to send some telegraph messages,' Leroy said. 'Find out more about this special train and what it's carrying.'

'You go take care of that, son.

Railroad hasn't told us anything about what might be coming through, so I'm not going to be much help until you enlighten me.'

'I ain't surprised about the railroad being close-mouthed. They tend to keep their business to themselves so nothing gets out,' LeRoy said.

'The feller we found back at that cabin was railroad,' Bodie said, 'so the railroad missed that. Looks like he was feeding McLennan information until they had their falling-out.'

'This McLennan sounds a hard feller.'

'He is,' LeRoy said. 'Smart. Organized. Likes to get his own way. Ty McLennan plays for keeps and doesn't like being taken for a fool.'

The marshal stepped out of the office, leaving Bodie with Conagher. 'You got plans?' Conagher said.

'Take a walk around town. See if I can pick up anything.'

'I might take a stroll down to the depot. Have a word with the local man in charge.'

'Don't give too much away about McLennan's bunch. There's no way of knowing if there are others on McLennan's payroll.'

'True enough,' Conagher said. 'I'll walk soft and just keep my eyes open.'

* * *

Roy Krupps woke from a restless sleep with an aching head and a sour taste in his mouth. He found he was in a hard bed in a shabby room, with daylight pushing in through a streaked window. There was a stale smell in the room, and he discovered the smell was coming from him. When he sat up, the pulsing ache in his head forced him to lie down again. He lay and cursed at his condition, at everyone and everything. His condition was a result of the whiskey he had drunk the night before. It wasn't the first time it had happened. Krupps liked his whiskey, but it always left its mark. When he sat up for the second time, it was with caution. He swung his legs off the bed and sat with his head resting in his hands, letting the room stop moving around him.

He recalled the saloon. The meal he had ignored and the glasses of whiskey. He recalled Bell suggesting they move somewhere else and walking out of the saloon. After that, his recall became distant. Eventually his memories became lost in a fog of confusion. He certainly couldn't remember ending up in bed.

That must have been down to Bell, his friend. He could always depend on Marty to look after him. It wasn't the first time and most likely wouldn't be the last. He and Bell had ridden too many trails, and their friendship was not to be broken.

Krupps thought about McLennan then. He was going to be mad at the way he had behaved. There was a lot riding on their visit to Junction City. If Krupps screwed things up, McLennan would be more than just mad. He had put in a lot of work; too much to let it be put at risk. His plan for the money train. The bank robbery at Clear Springs. The following trek across country and over the high divide to get them to Junction City. If all that was lost because he, Krupps, had put the plan off the rails . . . A harsh chuckle sounded. *Off the rails*. It might have been funny if it hadn't been serious.

Krupps got slowly to his feet, still feeling a little nauseous. He brushed absently at his wrinkled clothing. His hand touched his gunbelt, and he automatically checked to see if his gun was still in his holster. He found the smooth butt, the wooden grips cool against his fingers. Glancing around the bleak room, he saw his hat on the crooked nightstand, and moved on leaden feet to pick it up. There was water in the chipped jug. Krupps dunked his hand in and splashed tepid liquid over his face. He felt the rasp of his unshaven jaw and became aware of his unkempt condition. He splashed more water over his face. It helped a little. Krupps felt his stomach grumbling and recalled the steak meal he'd dismissed because he needed his whiskey. He felt in his pants pocket. His money was still there. He decided what he needed was food and some hot coffee. There was no mirror on the wall over the nightstand, and he figured that was most likely a good thing. The way he felt suggested the last thing he needed was to see how he looked. He jammed his hat on over his tangled hair and turned for the door.

*   *   *

The wagon was solidly built and high-sided, with a tied-down canvas cover over the support hoops. Mackie had it stored in a shed situated in the freight yard on the west side of town. The shed was padlocked and under the protection of the freight yard foreman. Mackie had paid the man well to see to it that the shed was not interfered with. He had been generous with his cash, promising the foreman, Andy Gregson, an equally generous amount when he came to collect his wagon. There was a risk involved, McLennan knew, but a certain degree had to be expected. Mackie understood how to handle men, his years in the military giving him mastery, and his choice of the foreman was not lacking. The man liked money too well to not follow through. When Mackie had taken McLennan to see the wagon and what it held, he found the shed untouched. The first thing he did was seek out the foreman and hand over the remainder of his watcher's fee. Gregson walked away happy.

With the doors closed, Mackie was finally able to show his prized Gatling gun. The supporting stand had been bolted to the solid bed of the wagon, the multi-barrel assembly turned so it was aimed out over the tailgate. Mackie had a small wooden crate next to the weapon. It was full of the long magazines that fed the .50 caliber cartridges into the top-load slot, giving Mackie a substantial amount of firepower.

'You stop that train,' Mackie said,

'and I'll keep the guards away. Turn 'em into shreds.'

'Can't fault a man who loves his work,' McLennan said.

Sanford looked away from the Gatling and said, 'There's something I feel nervous about, Ty.'

'What's that?'

'Mackie's yard foreman. Let's say he has a loose mouth tonight. Lets it slip he's come into money, and talks about the locked shed he'd been paid to watch over. What then, Ty?'

'He's got a point,' Bell said. 'He stayed quiet up to now, but Mackie has handed over the rest of his money. Maybe he won't be so eager to keep quiet.'

In the silence that followed, they thought over what Bell had said. The yard man might easily let something slip, intentionally or not, and it could arouse curiosity in the wrong quarters. The last thing they needed at this stage was to draw attention to themselves.

'You really trust that feller not to let something out?' McLennan said.

Mackie didn't have to say anything. His expression said it all.

Behind them a voice spoke up. 'I don't trust him,' Krupps said. 'Good thing I showed up.'

He had been standing there listening. Bell saw his partner ease into the shed. He looked the Gatling gun over, eyes bright as he took in the details of the weapon.

'You said it was something, Mackie. Never did figure you would be so damn right.' Krupps turned to McLennan. 'Ty, we cain't let this yard man stay loose. He says anything, and we're done for before we start. He needs quieting down. Now. Leave this with me. I'll catch up with you later.'

McLennan couldn't argue the point. 'Mackie, you point that feller out and let Roy handle it.'

'You sure you can deal with this?' Bell said.

'Damn right I can. I slept that whiskey off, so don't fret.'

They recovered the wagon, and Mackie

left the shed, Krupps on his tail. They made their way across the yard so that Mackie could point out the yard man.

'I got it now,' Krupps said.

Mackie made his way back to the shed where the others were waiting.

'We need to rent a couple of horses to pull the wagon,' McLennan said. 'Take our own animals and move out just before dark. We need to get into position by first light tomorrow. The money train is set to pass that ravine by mid-morning, according to the schedule Telford had. I don't want us not being there on time. If we miss this, we won't be getting a second money train showing up.'

Mackie and Bell headed for the livery. Inside the shed, Congrave set to readying his dynamite. He separated the bundle into smaller items, each with its own short fuse inserted. He would plant these in the chosen places as the train approached, and be ready.

Watching him carry out his preparations, Lee Sanford felt uncomfortable.

He did not favor being too close to the explosives, even though Congrave had told him the material was safe. Seeing the concerned look on his face made Congrave smile.

'Rest easy, friend,' he said. 'This is safe, take my word. It ain't about to go bang until I say so.'

Sanford nodded, still not entirely convinced.

★ ★ ★

Roy Krupps had made his way across the yard, keeping Gregson in sight. It wasn't difficult. The man was well built, running to fat, and he moved slowly. The area around the freight yard was busy, with workers moving back and forth. Freight cars on the tracks were constantly being loaded and unloaded, and no one took any notice of Krupps. He stayed well back from Gregson as the man stopped to speak with individuals.

Locomotives issued blasts of steam

and blew dark smoke from their stacks. The air was tainted by the smell from the wood- and coal-burners. Men called to each other as they worked. The sight of all the busy labor made Krupps smile to himself. He saw no pleasure in having to work for money. It was a damn sight easier — and a whole lot more profitable — to steal it. He was happy to let others do all the hard work.

After a half-hour, Gregson walked away from the freight yard, Krupps once again following, and headed towards town. He watched as Gregson cut across the lower end of the main street, making for the collection of shabby saloons, cafés and boarding houses that comprised the area. Following at a discreet distance, Krupps saw the man enter one of the boarding houses and had to quicken his steps, as he didn't want to lose sight of the man. He stepped up on the porch and went inside, peering through the door, and saw Gregson moving along the passage, pausing at a door. He opened it and stepped inside. Krupps waited until the door closed.

The house was silent. Krupps was aware he needed to finish what he was here for with as little disturbance as possible. There was risk, but the situation needed resolving now. He made his way to the door, pausing and listening. He could hear Gregson moving around inside the room. Krupps reached for his sheathed knife, drew it clear and reached for the handle. He eased the door open, slipped through and closed the door behind him.

Gregson stood with his back to Krupps, in the middle of the cheaply furnished single room. He had stripped off his coat, throwing it on the bed, and was in the act of removing his shirt. As he tugged the shirt off over his head, Krupps stepped in close and with a practiced move made a deep cut where the shape of Gregson's spine showed beneath his skin. The keen blade, expertly wielded, cut through flesh and severed the spinal cord. Gregson uttered a short grunt as he collapsed to the floor, a swell of blood flowing from the wound, streaming down the pale skin of his broad back. Bending over the man, Krupps hauled him onto his back. His blade made a second sweep across Gregson's exposed throat. The cut was wide and deep, laying the man's throat open. Blood surged thick and hot.

Krupps stepped back after he wiped the blade of his knife across the dying man's pants. He turned to the bed as he sheathed the knife, picking up Gregson's coat. It only took his a few seconds to locate the roll of cash Gregson had taken from Mackie. Krupps raised his hand in a mocking salute to Gregson, then stuffed the money in his own pocket.

'No use to you now,' he said.

He opened the door and peered into the corridor. Seeing it was empty, he walked back the way he had come, pausing before he stepped outside and back onto the street.

He was feeling pretty sure of himself until a voice called out behind him.

'Hold it, mister and turn around . . . '

* * *

Marshal Jim Conagher had asked around the freight yard, checking if anyone had seen Andy Gregson. It had occurred to him that the freight-yard foreman might be able to furnish him with information. He knew Gregson well enough to ask him questions about incoming special trains. Then again, even he might not have been advised about something as special as the money train. Conagher figured it was worth a few minutes of his time, even if it came to nothing.

He arrived at the freight yard only to be told that he had missed Gregson by a few minutes. Now he might have decided to leave it at that, but Conagher was a determined man, and once he had chosen a course of action he was inclined to follow it through. So he set off in the direction of Gregson's boarding house. It wasn't far; at the shabbier end of town. He knew that Gregson lived on his own and was known to be tight with his money. The boarding house where the man lived was cheap and basic, but Gregson was happy with what it provided.

Habit caused Conagher to slip off the hammer-loop, freeing the .45 caliber Colt Peacemaker. If anyone had ever asked him why, he would never come up with an answer. It had become a reflex action; something he did without thinking when he was on law business. He wasn't expecting Andy Gregson to do anything untoward. Even so, Conagher would admit, it was too late if something occurred and his weapon was tied down. The street was quiet as the lawman approached Gregson's boarding house.

A man had just walked out across the porch and stepped into the street. Nothing out of the ordinary, Conagher might have thought.

Until he spotted the blood spots marking the right leg of the man's pants. What caused Conagher's close inspection was the fact that those blood spots were glistening wet.

'Hold it, mister, and turn around.'

★ ★ ★

Krupps recognized the authority in the challenge. Before he began to turn, he knew he was going to see a man wearing a badge.

A goddam lawdog.

Sweet Jesus, that was all he needed.

He wasn't aware of the blood spots on his clothing. The question flashed through his mind as to why the law was calling him out. If he had been at his best, which he wasn't because of the previous night's drinking, Krupps might have thought differently. But all he could determine was the need to shut the man down. Right now he couldn't allow himself to be braced by this hick-town lawdog.

So Krupps began to turn around, his

right hand dropping towards the revolver holstered on his thigh. He ignored the slowness in his move, but convinced himself he could still best the lawman.

★ ★ ★

Bodie had left the livery stable, not having picked up any fresh news from Mayberry. He was angling across the open street, planning to catch up with Jim Conagher over at the freight yard.

He saw Junction City's lawman some way ahead of him, coming up behind a man who had just exited one of the cheap boarding houses. Conagher called out, left hand raised as he spoke.

The man ahead of him froze, then started to turn, his right hand going for the holstered gun on his right hip.

Conagher went for his own gun.

Two shots came.

Conagher stumbled back as he took a slug in his left side, twisting around as he went down. His own shot sent a slug into Krupps' left shoulder. He stumbled, cursing against the sudden pain.

Bodie ran forward, fisting his own weapon, hammer going back as he closed the distance. 'Hey,' he said, raising his voice so the word reached the man who had just shot Conagher.

Krupps, clamping a hand over his bleeding side, saw the tall figure striding towards him. 'Come on then,' he said. 'The hell with you all . . . ' He raised his gun, slower than he usually was, dogging back the hammer.

Bodie put three close shots into him, so fast the sounds merged into one. They smashed ribs as they went in deep. Krupps staggered, looking down at his body and seeing the blood pumping from it. He felt his legs collapse and then he was lying on the dusty street, tasting more blood as it burst from his throat. He looked up and saw the tall man stride past him, kicking his fallen gun out of reach. The man didn't even pause to look at Krupps as he went by.

Bodie crouched beside Conagher and

saw the spreading patch of blood down the lawman's side. 'There a doctor in this town?'

Conagher nodded. 'Doc Hazel. Good man.'

Bodie looked up as figures appeared. 'One of you go fetch Hazel,' he said. 'Do it now.'

Out of the corner of his eye, he saw a man break away from the crowd and run along the street.

'What was that all about?' Bodie said.

'I came to talk to Andy Gregson. He's railroad. Foreman at the yard. That feller stepped out of the boarding house. He had fresh blood on his pants. I told him to stop and he came out shooting. You go in and look for Gregson.'

Bodie told someone to stay with Conagher and crossed to step inside the boarding house. He checked doors as he walked along the corridor. When he stepped into Gregson's room and saw the state of the man's body, he didn't waste time going any further.

Junction City's doctor was kneeling

beside Conagher when Bodie got back outside.

'Gregson?'

'That feller got to him. And he won't be needing the doctor.'

Conagher sighed. 'What in hell is going on?'

'LeRoy and me . . . we're going to find out.' Bodie touched the doctor's arm. 'He going to be all right?'

'He will be after I dig that bullet out of him.'

Bodie pushed to his feet and watched as Conagher was lifted by a couple of men. They fell in behind the medic as he led the way to his office.

'Somebody needs to let the undertaker know about him and that feller Gregson,' Bodie said as he walked by the men standing around Roy Krupps' body.

★ ★ ★

Bell was ready to rush out and face down the man who had shot his partner

159

down. It took Mackie to hold him back.

'No,' McLennan said. 'We can still do this if we stay calm.'

'You see what they did to Roy? Shot him down like a dog in the street. Roy and me been together too long for me to let it lie.'

'Take it any further and we lose everything. Remember the plan, Marty. The money train. All that cash. Hell, we have it all set up. Nobody in town has to know why we're here. We stay peaceful. Slip out of Junction City and make the rendezvous. We get into position and wait. Marty, I'm sorry what happened to Roy. But it has, and there ain't a deal to be done — except carry on.'

Mackie felt Bell go slack, slumping in his grip. McLennan gave him a slight nod and Mackie relaxed his grip.

'Think there's still a chance we can do it?' Bell asked.

'We won't know if we quit,' Sanford said.

'We move out now,' McLennan said.

'Town will be busy over what happened just now. Mackie, go fetch the wagon team. Nice and quiet. No fuss. Once we have the wagon hitched, you roll it out and pick up the trail outside. Rest of us pick up our horses and ride out as well.'

Mackie walked up in the direction of the livery, making his way as casually as he could. He paid Mayberry for the rental and picked up the reins of the waiting team.

'Have 'em back in a couple of days, Mister Mayberry.' He nodded towards the open doors of the livery. 'Heard shooting a while back. Somebody said your marshal got hurt. He going to be all right?'

'I'm told he'll be laid up for a while.'

'Sorry to hear that.'

'At least we got that US marshal in town,' Mayberry said. 'He can keep an eye on things meantime. He come in with another feller. Big man, name of Bodie. Some kind of bounty man, I heard.'

'US marshal? You don't say. Hope things stay peaceful from now on.'

'Amen to that, Mister Mackie.'

'See you in a couple of days, soon as I deliver my freight.'

Mackie led the team out of the stable and along the street. When he reached the shed, he led them inside as the doors were opened. He set to harnessing the team to the wagon.

'You'll be interested to know there's a US marshal in town,' Mackie said.

'You think it's LeRoy?' Bell said.

McLennan shrugged his shoulders.

'Maybe that mountain boy didn't stop him after all,' Sanford said.

'What you all talkin' about?' Congrave said. 'This something else we should be worryin' about?'

McLennan shook his head. 'Let's go and pick up our horses. No reason we need to be fussed.'

They walked out of the shed and up to the livery. Inside they wasted no time readying their waiting horses. Mayberry watched quietly, as if there was something on his mind, until he made the connection.

'So where's the other feller who was with you? I recall him being an unsociable cuss.'

'Ain't with us any longer,' Bell said. His expression was bitter. His words snapped out with enough force to make Mayberry step back.

'Just . . . what with that stranger tangling with Jim Conagher and all. Could be it was . . . '

Bell rounded on him, anger bursting forth in a torrent. He grabbed Mayberry by his shirt and slammed him back against the side of the stall. 'You got a loose mouth . . . needs to be shut.'

His handgun came out of his holster and he slammed it against the side of the liveryman's head — two solid blows that drove Mayberry to his knees. Bell drove his boot into the man's side, and Mayberry slumped to the floor.

'Let's get the hell out of here,' McLennan said as they all mounted up.

They emerged from the livery and cut along the street. Despite the need to get clear of town, they managed to stay to a steady walk. At the far end of the street, they could see Mackie and the wagon. As he saw them, he gigged the team into motion.

★ ★ ★

It might have worked without a hitch if US Marshal Alvin LeRoy hadn't stepped into view as he left the town marshal's office and started across the street.

It could have worked if LeRoy, glancing at the riders, took a second look when he recognized one of them straight off.

Lee Sanford.

The black-gloved safe cracker. The man LeRoy knew from the past and who had been at Remford's place.

LeRoy didn't waste any more time. If he was looking at Sanford, then he was also facing Ty McLennan's bunch.

LeRoy went for his holstered gun, yelling out a warning over his shoulder. Bodie was following close, having picked up his rifle, and he acted fast when he heard LeRoy's call.

'McLennan.'

Bodie hit the boardwalk at a run, his Winchester already swinging up as he cleared the door. He took in the scene with a sweeping glance, seeing the mounted bunch going for their own weapons, caught off balance by LeRoy's appearance.

It was the marshal who fired first, his pistol snapping out a shot that planted a .45 slug in Marty Bell's shoulder. Bell slipped sideways in his saddle, hauling on his reins as his horse sidestepped in the wake of the shot.

In the seconds afterward, the street rang to the sound of multiple guns firing. Startled horses made accurate targeting difficult, and though Bodie and LeRoy acknowledged the fusillade, they were also aware none of the slugs had touched them.

LeRoy settled his gun again and put a second slug in Bell. This time his aim was true. Marty Bell shuddered at the impact of the heavy slug that struck him in the chest. He dropped from the saddle and thumped face down in the dust of the street.

Bodie had moved forward, his rifle to his shoulder now, and he laid his sights on the slim figure clad in a gray suit and black gloves. Lee Sanford, pulling his skittish horse back under control, fumbled his revolver from the high-ride holster he wore. He managed to lift it partway before Bodie's rifle cracked out three close .44–40 slugs. They hammered in through Sanford's coat and into his lean body. Ribs were shattered in an instant, the deformed slugs coring into his body and ripping his heart open. Sanford didn't have time to make any sound as he fell from his horse, one booted foot hooked in a stirrup. His horse, alarmed at the sudden weight pulling at it, kept moving, dragging Sanford through the dirt.

Mackie heard the outburst of firing and hauled the wagon to a halt. He scrambled from the seat and moved to the rear of the wagon. He tore open the canvas sheet hanging over the tailgate, exposing the Gatling. The weapon was already for use, and all Mackie had to do was crank the handle to fire.

'Get out of the way,' he said, his powerful voice carrying easily to his partners.

McLennan and Congrave heeled their horses to the side, leaving Mackie a clear field of fire.

Mackie understood things were going wrong, and if he didn't do something, matters could only get worse. So he did the only thing he could. His military training took over, and he faced the enemy and opened fire as McLennan and the others swung their horses aside.

The main street of Junction City erupted with sound as the Gatling's multi-barrels rotated and laid down a burst of deadly fire. The .50 caliber slugs pounded the ground, kicking up geysers of soil and stones. Mackie raised the trajectory, aiming for Bodie and LeRoy. The clatter of automatic fire split the air. It was fortunate for Bodie and the marshal that the Gatling had limited swivel ability due to being wagon-mounted.

Bodie took evasive action and stepped closer to the boardwalk, where he was able to raise his Winchester and take steady aim, trying to ignore the hard crackle of fire from the wagon-mounted weapon. LeRoy, lifting his Colt two-handed, sought a further target. They fired within seconds of each other.

The manhunter's rifle pumped out a trio of close-spaced shots, neatly placed into Mackie's right shoulder. The bulk of his body was concealed by the Gatling, and Bodie's shots knocked him clear of the weapon. The moment Mackie was in sight, Bodie triggered a couple more shots, the 44–40 slugs slamming into the man's body. Mackie stepped back and dropped to the bed of the wagon.

Alvin LeRoy's Colt, held firm, cracked twice. His aim was good, and considering he was firing on a man astride a horse gathering speed, accurate. Darren Congrave took both slugs through his upper body, one blowing out through his chest. He threw his arms wide, twisting in a convulsive movement before pitching from his saddle and hitting the ground with enough force to break bones.

McLennan turned his horse, facing back along the street, and triggered his handgun until it clicked on empty. There was a smirk on his face as he saw LeRoy drop to his knees, a spurt of blood from his left thigh as one of the outlaw's slugs struck him. McLennan sawed on his reins, dragging his horse away.

As Bodie skirted the now-silent wagon, snapping his rifle to his shoulder again to draw down on the fast diminishing Ty McLennan, his target spurred his horse out of sight as he reached the far end of the street, leaving Bodie frustrated and not a little angry at losing the man.

'Dammit all to hell,' he said. He turned abruptly, reaching LeRoy as the lawman struggled to his feet, one hand clamped over his bloody leg.

'Bodie,' LeRoy said, 'I'll survive. Get your damn horse and go after McLennan.'

Bodie yelled for someone to fetch the doctor.

'Do it,' LeRoy said. 'We can't let that bastard get away again.'

The aftermath of the conflict was going to keep LeRoy busy for some time, and he knew Bodie would pick up McLennan's trail easy enough. He would see it through to the end. LeRoy had no doubts on that score. It was what Bodie did. How he had built his reputation as the best.

It was why he was known as The Stalker.

* * *

Ty McLennan leaned across his horse's neck as he pushed it hard. He was seething with rage and disappointment — a boiling mix of emotions at the way

170

his long planning and organizing had been wiped away in such a short time. He tried to push it aside while he concentrated on the moment, and his need to get away from Junction City. Avoiding capture, or worse, catching a bullet, was what mattered most right now. The prize was out of reach. In fact, had never even been close. That damned pair had showed up and shattered his dream. Had taken the money train away from him. If he didn't keep moving, evading capture, his freedom would be lost as well. That meant far more than a fistful of dollar bills. If he ended up locked in a cell, he would have plenty of time to consider how it had all blown up in his face; snatched away before he had even made his attempt.

He had lost his crew as well.

Sanford the safe breaker.

Mackie and his machine gun.

The dynamite man Congrave.

Roy Krupps and Marty Bell, the men who had fought and ridden at his side for so long. They had sided with him through a variety of exploits; and though there had been times his patience had worn thin, Bell and Krupps had always been there for him.

McLennan was suddenly on his own. No one to back his plays. To share moments of peace. A meal over a campfire. A bottle of whiskey. From now on, he was going to have to keep his own company.

Sonofabitch.

Life had taken one hell of a twist. But in that moment of reflection, McLennan realized the most important thing right now was his survival. He had to put everything else out of his mind and concentrate on two things: staying alive and staying free. His priorities. Only a couple of small words. Yet their implications were massive. A nagging thought began to make itself known at that moment. It had to do with that freedom he was thinking about.

He had seen US Marshal LeRoy go down from his bullet.

The man siding with LeRoy — Bodie, the manhunter . . . If he had still been on his feet — and McLennan felt sure he had seen the tall figure remain upright — Bodie would be coming after him. He had no doubts on that. The man had a fearsome reputation. He was a dogged hunter, having built his long-standing reputation on never walking away. The talk was that Bodie never quit. He stayed on the hunt for as long as it took, and it was said he would bring his man back one way or another.

Dead or alive.

It would make no difference to Bodie.

McLennan urged his horse up a timbered slope, feeling the chill wind coming down off the higher peaks. He needed to gain the high levels, where he could check his back trail and see if he could spot any pursuit. It was important that he knew who was following him — how many were following him. A full posse, or just one man. Whichever it was, it didn't faze Ty McLennan. He was no coward. If it came to a standoff, he would put his back to the wall and shoot it out. If they figured he was going to quit meekly, there would be some surprises out there. Ty McLennan would go down fighting to his last bullet.

The moment he reached the high ground, McLennan reined in and swung out of the saddle, slipping his rifle from the sheath. He led his horse to the closest low-hanging branch and tied it. Then he walked to the crest of the slope and looked back the way he had come, eyes searching the terrain he had left behind. He had to search slowly, discarding shadows and dense thickets. He spent some long time doing so, aware that any pursuit, a single rider or a bunch, would be a distance away yet. He had ridden hard and fast since vacating Junction City so anyone following would be well behind. McLennan hunkered down on his heels, rifle across his thighs, patient as he waited for any sign.

It was quiet where he was apart from

the gentle soughing of the wind disturbing tree branches. Quiet enough so he could hear the labored breathing of his horse. He had pushed it hard since leaving the town behind, keeping up a relentless pace, and McLennan felt guilty about that. He would not have normally treated a horse in such a manner, but there had been little choice. He had needed to gain distance; to get himself well away from Junction City. And the only way open to him had been to drive his horse without regard to its well-being. For now, he was going to need time to let the animal rest.

McLennan stood and crossed to the horse. He leaned his rifle against the closest tree, unhooked one of his big canteens, and took off his hat to fill it with water. The horse turned its head and stared at the promise of water.

'Yeah, okay, horse, don't make me feel any worse than I already do,' he said.

He offered the hat, and the horse dropped its muzzle in and drank. It emptied the hat, lifted its head and shook it, sending a spray of water from its muzzle. With that done, it went back to cropping the grass at its feet.

McLennan took a swallow from the canteen, then hung it back on the horse. He picked up his rifle and went back to where he had been standing before, then dropped the damp hat on the ground to let it dry out. Next he checked his back trail and sank down on his heels again.

He had only been searching for a couple of minutes before he spotted movement: a single horse and rider, moving slow and steady. McLennan watched the rider clear cover and angle across a small grassy meadow. He kept watch, searching for any other riders. There were none. The rider was on his own.

And that convinced McLennan he was being tracked by the manhunter.

Bodie was on his trail.

Moving slow. Most likely set on following McLennan's tracks.

McLennan gripped his rifle, fingers itching to make his rifle sing. He pushed back on his thought. His target was way, way out of range, and would be for some time yet. Bodie had his tracks to follow. He had no immediate need to rush his pursuit. When he read the tracks left by McLennan's horse, Bodie would see by the hoof-print spacing that McLennan had been riding hard, his mount pounding the earth as it sped along. He would know that eventually McLennan would have to rest his animal. The uneven terrain would not become any easier, and if McLennan was heading for higher ground, his overstretched horse was going to need rest.

Feeling a need to reassure himself, McLennan checked both his weapons. It was a redundant move because he had reloaded shortly after leaving Junction City. He admitted the situation was getting to him. Beyond losing his planned strike at the money train and the loss of his people, he now had

Bodie on his back trail.

Damned if that wasn't the worst thing.

McLennan picked up on the distant rider. Still coming on, slow but sure. Still out of rifle range.

McLennan gripped his rifle hard until his knuckles popped under the tension — a sure sign he was allowing the pressure to unsettle him, which was not something that happened to Ty McLennan often. Staying calm was something he prided himself on. Yet right now, after the unexpected turn of events, he was beyond being calm. He was getting angry slowly, allowing his feelings to morph into something that built as he watched Bodie's distant form move ever closer. McLennan focused on the man, making him the center of his blossoming rage. A small part of him was telling him it was a foolish thing to do.

Anger and rage only took away his control, and might easily push him into doing something reckless. He needed to be steady. The trouble was, the more he thought about Bodie, the stronger his anger became. He had to stop the man. With Bodie dead, he would be able to ride away safely. Put distance between himself and Junction City. Ride far without the nagging feeling someone was dogging him.

McLennan stood, went to his horse and caught the reins. He didn't take to the saddle, but simply walked the horse to give it some extra freedom from his weight.

The hell with you, Bodie. Just keep coming. We'll have our time soon enough.

ACROSS THE HIGH DIVIDE

Seeing the lone rider reach the high slope and spend some time there, watching his back trail, Bodie knew he had been spotted. He kept moving, knowing he was still well out range of even a rifle. It made no difference if McLennan was a good shot. Out of range meant just that. No 44–40 could reach Bodie yet. The slug would drop to earth before it could touch him. If he kept moving, closing the distance, he might put himself in danger, but Bodie didn't believe McLennan would stay where he was for too long. The man was on his own now. He had no backup. His bunch was finished, dead and gone. His elaborate scheme to rob the money train had been wiped out before it really had a chance. Ty McLennan was bound to be a tad upset at that; and when a man lost the way

McLennan had, a degree of agitation was bound to set in.

If Bodie was any judge of character, McLennan would be angry at the way his plan had gone astray. Depending on how he handled that, McLennan might set himself the task of settling with Bodie. On the other hand, he could very well shrug it all off and concentrate on getting himself clear out of the territory to some place where he was not known and spend his time working on a fresh scheme. There was no way of knowing, and Bodie didn't waste too much time trying to figure it.

He had a simple goal in mind. That was to catch up with Ty McLennan and work out his personal score. For Bodie, there was no kind of problem with that. He held his thoughts easy. Right or wrong, he wanted Ty McLennan under his gun. There would be those who recoiled at the thought of vengeance as a justified motive. As far as Bodie was concerned, they could have their opinions, just as long as they didn't interfere in his life. Every time he thought about Gunnar Olsen, he felt the feelings raise themselves again. Olsen, his friend, had died because McLennan broke his trust. Killing the unarmed lawman had been nothing more than the callous act of a pitiless man. Olsen's life had meant nothing to McLennan. He had wiped it out in an instant and had ridden out of Clear Springs without another thought.

Bodie pulled his horse to a stop and sat staring up the long, high slope separating him from the man he was following.

For some time, they both remained still, each with his own thoughts. And it was uppermost in their minds that they wanted the other dead.

It was McLennan who moved first, taking up his reins and easing into the saddle, turning away from the top of the slope and moving on. He rode out of sight.

Bodie eased himself in his saddle and patted his horse along its neck. 'Looks like we have us a long climb, feller. We'll take it easy; let that sonofabitch get well ahead. Something tells me he's going to keep moving. We'll let him do that. Keep our distance until we figure it's the time. Then we'll deal with Mister Ty McLennan — you can bet your next round of oats on that.'

The way became steeper as Bodie climbed towards the higher ground. He let the horse find its own way, picking a path that wound through the clumps of brush and brittle grass. Loose rocks littered the surface. Bodie picked up on McLennan's trail, the hoof prints clear, as well as tramped-down plants. McLennan had made no attempt to hide his path. He knew Bodie was following and knew where he was, so wasting time concealing his passing would have been a fruitless exercise. McLennan wanted to gain distance, not conceal himself.

Reaching the spot where he had last seen McLennan, Bodie noticed the lengthening shadows. The day was starting to fade. He felt a rising wind as well, turning his face skywards, and saw a mass of dark cloud spreading across the sky to the west. He hunched in the saddle, tugging his hat down snug as the breeze played at the curled brim. The signs were for more rain. There was no escaping the fact. Up here in the high country, with the brooding slopes and rocky escarpments, the weather was unrepentant. It changed at will.

'Hoss, we're going to get wet again.'

The only good thing about it was that McLennan would be going through it as well. Any discomfort would be shared with the outlaw, and Bodie took a peevish amount of satisfaction at the thought.

A sudden swirl of wind hit him. His horse balked for a moment. It had picked up on the weather change and made its feelings known as the first drops of rain reached them. Bodie hauled it to a halt, reaching to unfurl his slicker from behind his saddle. He pulled it on, spreading it down his body. He pulled his hat down tighter, muttering his displeasure.

The rainfall increased, cold against his exposed face. The darkening clouds served to hasten the failing light. To add to the misery, Bodie picked up the rumble of thunder.

'Hell, all we need now is lightning.'

He regretted the thought some little time later when the bright flashes started to split the sky. For a fleeting moment, the thought crossed Bodie's mind: *What the hell am I doing up here?* It was a notion brought on by the situation and the inclement weather, and Bodie felt a moment of regret that he had allowed it to intrude. He knew why he was here.

It was for Gunnar Olsen. No more, no less. A trek across the divide for his friend. The moment passed, and Bodie offered a silent apology for briefly allowing his physical weakness to override his sense of loyalty to Gunnar.

The scenery stood out as the lightning flashed, bathing everything in stark white. The jagged streaks of energy, crackling with nature's power, made Bodie haul back on his horse's reins as the animal reacted. It might have panicked if his strong hands had not pulled its head down.

He needed to find shelter. The day was close to coming to an end, and Bodie didn't want to be caught out in a bad storm. Taking in the immediate area, he chose the mass of trees close by and angled the horse towards the timber. When he reached the fringe of the trees, he dismounted and led the animal under cover. The close-growing trees formed a sheltering canopy overhead, but the rising wind still managed to filter through.

Bodie moved deeper in, partially sheltered from the rain and wind, knowing it was going to be a long, uncomfortable night. There was nothing he could do about that, so he would a find a place and sit out the storm, hoping it might blow itself clear of the area. He reached a place he considered the closest to a shelter and led his horse in: a high rise of rock that formed a hump some twenty feet across and ten high, with a growth of mossy green covering it and tangled brush spreading over the sides. He moved around the mound until he reached where the cut of the wind was mostly blocked off. It was the best spot he was going to find. Bodie tied the reins to a thick growth of brush, patting the horse along its neck.

'No warm stall tonight, son,' he said. 'Not for either of us.'

He searched in his saddlebag pouch and pulled out a couple of strips of jerky. That and his canteen of water were going to be his meal for the night. He retreated until he found a likely spot, sat with his back to the rock with his slicker tucked around him, and hunched over. As he chewed on the tough meat and washed it down with water, he found he was thinking about the meals he had shared with Ruby Keoh . . .

Neatly dressed in a suit and string tie, freshly shaved and enjoying the company, he had eaten the well-cooked steak and accompanying side dishes with gusto. A bottle of wine, chosen by Ruby, had gone down well. In the comfort of a hotel dining room, lamp lit, in the company of the young woman, Bodie had been as close to heaven as he was liable to get while still on the living side. After the main meal, there had been some refreshing dessert, which he had trouble recalling, followed by fresh coffee. It was a long mile away from how he normally ate. Bodie took his pleasure as and when it came, and being seated across from Ruby only added to the occasion. She was a pleasant companion, never short of something to say and always presenting a welcome distraction. The problem was, those moments were few and far between; so Bodie made a promise to himself that he would endeavor to alter that situation when the chance next arose . . .

The memories only bit deep as he stared out into the surrounding dark, listening to the wind battering the trees and the rain sluicing from the thundery sky. Lightning cracked and hissed, white-hot as it illuminated his current situation.

'Damn it to hell and back,' Bodie said. 'Sooner I get this done, the better.'

He found a half-smoked thin cigar in his shirt pocket and drew it out from under the slicker. He thumbed a match alight and got the cigar burning. The wavering flame from the match made him wish he had a fire going. Bodie knew there was little chance of that, not with the rain-soaked wood. It was not an impossibility, but the chances were slim, and he wasn't in the mood to struggle with the effort. He smoked his cigar down to the nub, pulled his hat low, and thought some more about Ruby Keoh.

Twice during the night he was disturbed by rumbles of thunder and the occasional streaks of lightning. When he woke, it was to rain still falling, coaxed into slanting sheets by the ever-present wind. Bodie roused his reluctant horse and climbed into the saddle, then turned the animal out of the trees and resumed his line of travel. He was not in the best of humor. He would have welcomed a hot bath, followed by a hot meal and clean clothes. None of those showed on the immediate horizon.

His thoughts turned to the man he was following, wondering how McLennan had spent the night. Cold and wet, he hoped. Ty McLennan deserved any discomfort he received. Petty as it sounded, Bodie allowed himself the indulgence as he pushed on.

★   ★   ★

Ty McLennan sat back on his heels, staring at the motionless form of his dead horse. He forgot his own aching body, focusing on the still shape, unable to believe his run of misfortune that had started with the disaster at Junction City and culminated in the death of his horse.

It had been down to his own stupidity. Determined to maintain his lead over Bodie, McLennan had pulled out of the shelter he had found to sit out the storm-riven night as soon as light began to show. Rain was still beating down from the higher slopes, drenching the ground and creating numerous water spills. In his haste to move on, McLennan had pushed his mount hard — too hard, it turned out, when the horse had missed its footing on a muddy stretch awash with rain. The soft mud had simply given way under the horse's weight, pitching it sideways. In a flurry of motion, horse and rider went down heavily, loose earth sliding away from the edge of the path they were taking. McLennan realized the danger as his horse gave a shrill scream and they tumbled over the edge.

He left the saddle, unable to do a thing to prevent the fall. His breath was driven from him as he hit the slope, his forward motion flinging him down. He seemed to be moving for a long time, dazed and struggling to draw air into his lungs. Even when he stopped moving, body pulsing with pain, he felt the frustration of yet another mishap holding him back.

'Dumb as a pair of socks, Ty,' he said. 'Damn fool play is going to give Bodie his chance.'

McLennan stumbled to his feet, rubbing at his left shoulder where he had landed hard. He spotted his hat lying on the sodden ground and snatched it up. Jamming it on his head, he caught sight of his horse a few yards away. It lay in an odd sprawl, not moving, nor making any sound. When he reached it, he realized the horse wasn't even breathing. The way its head lay twisted, almost bent double against its neck . . . He didn't need to look any closer. The horse was dead.

McLennan sank down on his heels, quietly cursing his continuing streak of bad luck. It did not help as he accepted he had been partly to blame, pushing his horse when he should have been riding with caution. But he still felt misfortune was really making a go of it. How could one man have so much go wrong in such short a time?

Pushing to his feet, McLennan leaned over the horse and loosened the strings holding his saddlebags secure. It took him a couple of minutes to free the pouch caught under the horse's carcass. He carried his spare ammunition in the bags. More importantly, there was also the remainder of the money taken from the Junction City bank. The way his luck was running, McLennan was going to need the cash. He needed a fresh mount, and he might have to buy one if he couldn't steal one. His horse lay on its left side, so he was able to slide his rifle from the saddle boot. His canteen was trapped under the dead weight and so was his possibles bag. He didn't fret over the loss too much. Right now he wasn't about to suffer from dehydration, not with the rain still falling; and Ty McLennan had gone without food many times.

He checked under his slicker. His

handgun was still in its holster, and he had a knife sheathed on his belt. If Bodie came, he would have to face an armed man ready to fight if he needed to. It would most likely come to that, because the manhunter had a tenacious nature and wasn't one to give up on a wanted man. On the other side of the coin, Ty McLennan wasn't the kind to quit easily.

Saddlebags slung over his shoulder, rifle in his left hand, McLennan stumbled his way up the slope until he was on level ground again. This time he didn't waste time looking back. He knew Bodie was behind him, driven by his determination to catch his man.

Then it occurred to McLennan that Bodie had a horse. He'd let that slip, but with it coming into his thoughts he saw a chance to get hold of a fresh mount. If he could do that, a greater part of his current problem would vanish.

'Sonofabitch,' he said. 'Might not be such a bad day after all.'

He moved off, trudging across the soaked and muddy ground, his eyes searching the way ahead for a likely spot where he could lay in wait for Bodie to appear.

Ty McLennan ain't throwing in his hand, Bodie. One way or another, I'm going to pick that winning card and cash you out.

★   ★   ★

From what Bodie could figure, McLennan and his horse had been caught in runoff coming down from the higher elevation. A closer inspection told him the horse had broken its neck in the fall. He noticed that McLennan's saddlebags and rifle were missing. The man had survived the fall, collected his belongings and moved on. Climbing back up to where his own horse stood, Bodie looked around for tracks McLennan might have left behind. He wasn't hopeful he would find anything. The continuous downpour was liable to have washed away any boot prints. Even so, Bodie led his horse as he scanned the ground. He didn't find anything, but he was certain McLennan would be moving in the direction he had been taking before losing his own horse. If he stayed on course, he would eventually clear the slopes of the divide and start to descend to the flatlands below. There would be settlements down there. Towns McLennan would want to reach. Bodie was trying to put himself in the man's boots.

The man needed a saddle under him. He was not going to get too far on foot. And Ty McLennan was the kind of man who would do whatever he needed to restore his former position, regardless of who he challenged in order to do just that. The thought had come to Bodie that McLennan, with his agile mind, would have considered the fact that the man following him possessed a horse. If he was able to deal with Bodie, getting him off his hands, he would be in the position of taking the manhunter's mount. With that thought lodged firmly in Bodie's mind, caution moved up a couple of notches.

Bodie kept moving, his eyes searching ahead and to the sides. Now he was looking at a possible, even likely, ambush — a shot coming at him from concealment. McLennan had taken his rifle when he had left his horse. It offered him the advantage of being able to take cover and wait for Bodie to walk into his sights. The thought did not sit happily with Bodie. Given the choice, he would take facing a man in the open over having to deal with a hidden threat. Here, though, the choice had been taken away from him; and if he was right, McLennan was going to stay in the shadows and attempt to put Bodie down from concealment.

Ignoring the constant downpour bouncing against his slicker and soaking his hat, Bodie stayed on track. He slid his right hand under the folds of the enveloping garment and loosened the holstered Colt, slipping off the hammer loop. He held the reins in his left hand, cradling his rifle in the crook of his left arm. The feeling grew that McLennan would be close now. He would have lost time dealing with the aftermath of his fall. Bodie was closing the distance, constantly examining the terrain, searching for places he would have considered likely ambush points. The rainfall cut down his ability to see far. The only saving grace there was that it would restrict McLennan as well.

Off to Bodie's left, a stream swollen by the heavy rain surged and roiled, the water brown from loosened earth. It was breaching the banks, water spreading across the ground. Bodie's boots splashed through the runoff. As he felt himself stumble, his right foot sinking into a depression hidden by the water, he felt the tug of a shot as a slug ripped through the folds of his slicker.

He let go of the reins, dropping to the ground as the crack of the shot reached him; and out of the corner of his eye he saw the brief muzzle flash off to his right.

Bodie's horse, startled by the sound of the shot, pulled aside. It left him totally exposed for long seconds. Flat down, Bodie snapped his Winchester to his shoulder, his mind's eye still focused on the spot where the shot had come from. He triggered and fired once, then a couple more times, then gathered his legs under him and took off running for a hump of grassy earth. As he flopped into cover, the other rifle fired again, sending multiple shots in his direction. Bodie could hear the slugs thumping into the top of the hump.

He levered a fresh load into the Winchester, then dropped the rifle to the ground and dragged the restricting folds of the slicker over his head, losing his hat in the process. Free of the slicker, he snatched up his rifle and crawled to one end of the hump, peering round to focus on the spot where the shooter had been concealed. He saw a tangle of brush; a stand of timber. If that was where McLennan was concealed, he had himself a prime location. It was higher than Bodie's cover, allowing McLennan the advantage of being able to see a wider area.

Bodie's horse had drifted away, now content to graze on the grass. Seeing the horse must have been a tempting draw for McLennan. It was the prize he was aiming for, there was no doubt in Bodie's mind. He also realized how close he had come to taking McLennan's bullet. That misstep had saved his life.

Bodie lay for a moment, feeling the cold rain soak through his clothing. Off to the north, thunder still rumbled. The sky still held dark banks of heavy cloud, and the storm showed no signs of easing up.

Movement amongst the timber caught his attention — a dark figure flitting between trees. Bodie aimed and fired, and saw his slug rip a wedge of wood from the trunk, bark flying. The figure returned fire and a gout of earth flew in the air, smearing the side of Bodie's face. The clammy feel of the dirt did more to galvanize Bodie into action. He laid a pair of shots in McLennan's direction and saw the figure jump back, then pushed himself upright, angling across the slope as he closed on the outlaw's position.

Damn fool move, he told himself. *Liable to get you shot.*

He knew his move was reckless. It made no difference. Bodie kept going, zigzagging as he raced up the slope, slamming in his heels to keep himself from slipping on the rain-soaked ground. His rifle cracked with sound as he laid down more shots in McLennan's direction. Wood chips flew. Brass shell casings spun in the air.

Ty McLennan stepped into view, taken aback by Bodie's wild charge. He made to level his own weapon and partly succeeded before one of Bodie's slugs whacked into his rifle, impacting against the metal receiver. The rifle was wrenched from McLennan's grasp, numbing his hands for a moment.

Bodie triggered another shot — his hammer falling on an empty breech. He launched the rifle at McLennan.

McLennan slapped the Winchester aside. Bodie slammed into him, the force of his solid body knocking McLennan backwards. He crashed against a tree, his breath driven from him. He stood frozen as Bodie swung his right fist forward, smashing it against McLennan's jaw. The blow spun McLennan aside, Bodie following with another punch that opened a gash across McLennan's left cheek. It sluiced blood down his face.

The sudden pain jolted McLennan, and he swung a fist that caught Bodie across the mouth, tearing flesh. McLennan dropped a hand to claw his own slicker aside to get to his handgun. Bodie lunged at him, using his body strength to push McLennan back, and hammering more blows to the man's face. McLennan drove his knee at Bodie's groin, and though it landed, the force of the blow was lessened by the folds of his slicker. They grappled for a moment, hands seeking to take hold, twisting as they struggled. Taking a handful of wet slicker, Bodie brought his right fist around in a powerful blow that cracked against the side of McLennan's jaw, snapping his head around, blood spraying from his mouth. The brute force of the blow sent McLennan stumbling back, but with his hands still knotted in Bodie's coat. They slid off balance together, the slick ground underfoot letting them slide; and, clinging at each other, they fell in a fighting tangle down the slope.

Hitting bottom, they broke apart, McLennan shedding his own slicker as he pushed to his feet and met Bodie head on. They were both solid, rawhide tough men, and their clash would have stopped many in their tracks. Fists swung, making contact with telling effect. Neither man went for their holstered guns now. They were determined to make this a personal fight.

McLennan, the thwarted outlaw, driven by the knowledge that his long-planned scheme to take the money train had been destroyed by Marshall LeRoy and Bodie, wanted payback.

Bodie needed McLennan to pay for what he had done to his friend Gunnar Olsen. Vengeance. Revenge. A reckoning. Call it what you wanted, Bodie had decided, but Ty McLennan was not going to walk away from what he had done. He had killed Gunnar simply because the man, who was the law in Clear Springs, had trusted him. Had given the man a job that allowed him to walk into the town's bank and steal from it. Taken in by McLennan's smooth manner, Gunnar Olsen had given him the opportunity to carry out the first step of his plan to rob the money train outside Junction City.

McLennan stumbled under Bodie's relentless attack; but throwing out his own solid fists, he landed several telling blows to face and body, including a savage blow to Bodie's side, over his ribs. The manhunter stepped back, sucking in a breath as a dull pain flared. Badly bruised, maybe even with cracked bones, he absorbed the blow and looped a powerhouse response that crunched against McLennan's left cheek. Flesh split and more blood streamed down the outlaw's face. He staggered, sent off balance by the sheer force of the blow. He felt the inside of his cheek forced against his jaw, loosening teeth, a harsh sound bursting from his lips. Blood flooded the inside of his mouth, spilling from his lips.

The pain from the injuries spurred McLennan into sudden action, and he went for his gun. When he made to lift it, the hammer loop, still in place, prevented him from drawing. Instinct made him snatch at the knife sheathed on his belt, sliding it free with his left hand and slashing at Bodie. It was a reckless move and Bodie was able to avoid it, his own right hand crossing to his left side and freeing his own blade.

McLennan stepped back, his expression changing to one of concern, his eyes fixed on the brutal-looking knife in Bodie's grasp. Ty McLennan was no beginner when it came to using a knife, though he did his best to avoid fighting with one. He just didn't favor hand-to-hand combat. Right now, however, he had no choice. The way Bodie moved and handled his own knife told McLennan he was facing someone who knew how to perform with a blade.

He made an attempt at freeing his Colt again, fingers touching the rawhide loop. Bodie feinted, his blade flashing in and opening a deep cut across the back of McLennan's hand. Flesh parted and blood gushed from the gaping wound as McLennan moved back, making wild slashes with his own knife. A degree of panic set in. The wound Bodie had opened left his hand immobile, his fingers suddenly numb and dangling uselessly.

'Sonofabitch,' he said.

Bodie, face expressionless, stayed silent, his gaze fixed rigidly on McLennan. He moved almost leisurely, the deadly blade of his knife cutting back and forth as he circled his opponent.

Blood was streaming down his face from the punches McLennan had landed, streaking his flesh with red. His left eye showed dark bruising as well, but he seemed able to shrug off his personal injuries as he made a concerted effort and slapped aside McLennan's knife hand, bringing his own blade in with a powerful sweep that sliced across his opponent's torso, cutting from right to left.

The move was too fast for McLennan to even register until he felt the beginning of pain. The awful sensation was followed by a bloody flood, his flesh parting, the wound gaping deep and wide. McLennan dropped his gaze and watched in horror as his organs, released by the great wound, spilled out in a mass. He dropped to his knees, letting go of the knife, and saw Bodie step away from him, sheathing the big knife.

'That was for Gunnar Olsen,' Bodie said. Then he freed his own Colt, dogged back the hammer and put a single .45 caliber slug between McLennan's eyes. The impact snapped McLennan's head back, the slug coring in deep and blowing out the back of his skull. 'And that was for me.'

Bodie made his way back up the slope. He saw the saddlebags McLennan had dropped and took them with him as he went to collect his horse. He rested against the animal as a feeling of nausea rolled over him. The ache in his side was growing stronger now. After a time he draped the saddlebags across the front of his saddle, picked up his sodden hat and jammed it on his aching head. Then he retrieved the rifle he had dropped, sliding it into the scabbard, and dragged himself slowly back into the saddle.

He sat for a while, ignoring the rain still falling from the lead-colored sky, and thought about picking up the slicker he had discarded. But even the effort of thinking about it made him wearier, and he muttered to himself about 'the hell with it' and rode away.

He picked up his trail, turning the horse, and let it make its own pace for the ride back to Junction City. He hurt from head to foot, felt dog-tired, and not for the first time wondered why he put himself through it all each time he took up a chase.

But this time had been different. He had tracked Ty McLennan and his bunch for a reason apart from monetary reward. He wasn't feeling particularly virtuous. Had no pretense of nobility.

He had done it simply because Gunnar Olsen had been a friend, one of the few Bodie actually had. That made all the difference.

* * *

When he rode into Junction City, half-way through a cloudy day, Bodie was hanging on to his saddle through sheer stubbornness. He brought his equally weary horse to a stop outside the jail, ignoring the curious stares from the towns-folk. He slid from the saddle, aching fingers looping the reins around the rail. He took the saddlebags from where they had sat all through his ride, slid his Winchester free, and stepped up to the jail door. He pushed it open and stepped inside.

Alvin LeRoy, seated behind the desk, glanced up and couldn't hold back the look of concern on his face. 'Hell, Bodie, I won't say I'm not surprised,' he said.

Bodie slumped into one of the chairs fronting the desk, dropping his saddle-bags and rifle to the floor. 'You got any coffee on the go?'

LeRoy pushed to his feet, favoring his left leg, leaning on a walking stick as he limped his way across to the stove and the simmering pot. He filled an enameled mug and handed it to Bodie.

'Ain't a nice way of saying it, Bodie, but you look like hell on a bad day.'

Bodie's face was a discolored mask, with bruises and cuts across it. His left eye was still swollen. A few days' stubble added to his unkempt appearance.

'Nice to be back, Alvin.'

Carrying his own mug back to the desk, LeRoy sat down with obvious satisfaction. He stared at Bodie for a time before he spoke. 'You get it done?'

Bodie simply nodded. 'Tell you about it later. I need a couple of things first. Have someone see to my horse. It deserves the best. Then I need to have the doc look at my side. I figure I might have bruised ribs, mebbe even cracked.'

LeRoy hauled himself upright again and crossed to the door, where he caught someone going by and passed on Bodie's needs. Before he sat down again, he leaned on his stick. 'Anything else 'fore I sit?'

'No.' Bodie watched the marshal as he moved to regain his seat. 'That leg giving you some grief?'

'Only when I have to keep getting up and moving around.'

Bodie managed a thin smile. He swallowed the hot coffee and let the tension ease. 'You taken over from Conagher?'

'Only 'til he gets back on his feet.

That bullet he took turned out to be a sight worse than expected. On top, he picked up a fever, so the doc ordered him to stay abed until he comes through.' LeRoy indicated the paperwork spread across the desk. 'I got enough reports here to keep me occupied for a coon's age.'

'I'd give you a hand,' Bodie said. 'Only I'm no great help when it comes to paperwork. To be honest, all I want right now is a bath followed by bed.' He indicated the saddlebags. 'Don't know how much money there is, but I figure McLennan was carrying the rest from the robbery in Clear Springs. They'll be happy to get it back.'

'Every one of the McLennan bunch was carrying rolls of cash,' LeRoy said. 'I'll put it all together and get it back to the Clear Springs bank.' He watched Bodie for a moment. 'Do we figure this came out right? McLennan and his bunch accounted for. Stolen money back.'

Bodie finished his coffee and placed

the mug on the desk. 'Not entirely,' he said.

LeRoy didn't need to say anything. He understood what Bodie was getting at. Even after everything that had happened, Gunnar Olsen was still dead.

And that, for Bodie, was the worst part of the whole affair.

Books by Neil Hunter
in the Linford Western Library:

INCIDENT AT BUTLER'S STATION

BODIE:
TRACKDOWN
BLOODY BOUNTY
HIGH HELL
THE KILLING TRAIL
HANGTOWN
THE DAY OF THE SAVAGE
DESERT RUN

BRAND:
GUN FOR HIRE
HARDCASE
LOBO
HIGH COUNTRY KILL
DAY OF THE GUN
BROTHERHOOD OF EVIL
LEGACY OF EVIL
DEVIL'S GOLD
THE KILLING DAYS
CREOLE CURSE

We do hope that you have enjoyed reading this large print book.

Did you know that all of our titles are available for purchase?

We publish a wide range of high quality large print books including:
Romances, Mysteries, Classics
General Fiction
Non Fiction and Westerns

Special interest titles available in large print are:
The Little Oxford Dictionary
Music Book, Song Book
Hymn Book, Service Book

Also available from us courtesy of Oxford University Press:
Young Readers' Dictionary
(large print edition)
Young Readers' Thesaurus
(large print edition)

For further information or a free brochure, please contact us at:
Ulverscroft Large Print Books Ltd.,
The Green, Bradgate Road, Anstey,
Leicester, LE7 7FU, England.
Tel: (00 44) **0116 236 4325**
Fax: (00 44) **0116 234 0205**

Other titles in the
Linford Western Library:

COFFIN FOR AN OUTLAW

Thomas McNulty

When legendary lawman-turned-bounty-hunter Chance Sonnet reappears, the word spreads that he wants Eric Cabot dead. Cabot, in the dark as to Sonnet's motives, sends his men to kill Sonnet first — but the task proves more difficult than he imagines. Sonnet also finds himself pursued by a plucky newspaperwoman and an old Texas Ranger who knows something of his past. Blazing a trail in a buckboard and hauling a pine coffin intended for Cabot, Chance Sonnet is a man haunted by the past and facing a future steeped in blood.

A TOWN CALLED INNOCENCE

Simon Webb

Falsely convicted of murder and sentenced to hang, it seems as though the end of young Will Bennett's life is in sight — but a strange circumstance of fate frees him to track down the real murderer. His journey takes him to a Texas town where he learns the truth about the plot that nearly sent him to the gallows. Bennett's journey from the town called Innocence to the final showdown with the man who framed him for murder ends in a bloody shootout, from which only one man will emerge alive.